# Family Lies
## And Other Stories

Iris Carden

Family Lies: And Other Stories
Published by: Iris Carden
             Ipswich, QLD, Australia.
             iriscardenauthor.net

Cover Art: Bleeding Rose by Iris Carden
ISBN: 978-0-6459679-0-6
A catalogue record for this work is available from the National Library of Australia.

# ContentsFamily Lies

## Other Stories

# Author's Note

*For many years, my former rheumatologist encouraged me to write a book about someone with lupus. Sadly, he died before I came up with a story with an ideal character to share my condition. I hope he would have liked my story.*

*The main story in this book is Family Lies is a story of a woman who has been through a rough life, but is now settled, with everything she needs and wants.*

*For her, the only downsides are that her lupus, her mother's dementia, and an annoying ex-husband.*

*Her otherwise idyllic life is disrupted by a note that says, "Give me my money bitch, or else."*

*From there, things escalate, and putting everyone she loves in danger.*

*Apart from Family Lies, there are ten short stories in this book, selected to loosely fit the theme of family. There are some stories of love, some of betrayal, some of absolute absurdity.*

# Family Lies
## Chapter 1: The Message

Emily looked at the sphygmomanometer cuff Jenny was wrapping around her upper arm.

"You know, I could do this myself," she said.

"And yet you pay a live-in nurse."

"Mostly to look after my mother."

"Your mother's not all that sick. She just has dementia. I could do her care in two half hour visits a day. Stop complaining, and let me do some work. Your blood pressure's up. That's from arguing with me. Arguing with your nurse is not good for you. Finger prick now."

Emily obediently held out her hand for the blood glucose test.

"That's all good," Jenny said. "How about you get in the pool for your hydrotherapy."

"How about you stop bossing me around?"

"I can't. Bossing you around is what you pay me the big bucks for. Now be a cooperative patient and get down to the pool."

Emily's housekeeper Carole knocked on the door of Emily's sitting room. "Sorry to bother you. I checked the mail as I came in. Normally, I'd put it on your desk, but this is concerning. I thought you'd want to see it right away."

Emily took the piece of paper, which was not in an envelope, and apparently torn from a notepad. Written on it in a semi-legible capitals were the words: "GIVE ME MY MONEY BITCH OR ELSE".

All three women looked at it.

"I think that needed a comma after 'bitch' and an exclamation mark at the end," Emily said dismissively.

"Aren't you worried about it?" Carole asked.

"I think you should take it seriously," Jenny answered.

"Why? I know I don't owe anyone any money. If they really thought I owed them anything, they should have sent me an invoice, or at least said who they were and what they thought I owed. Surely whoever this is doesn't think I'm psychic."

"Still," Jenny said, "there's an implied threat there. Maybe you should report it to the police."

"And tell them what? Someone sent me a nasty letter?"

"If we check the security footage, we might find out more," Jenny said.

Emily checked her phone for the feed from the front gate camera. The note had been dropped in the letter box just after 6am by someone in blue jeans, a grey hoodie, and a disposable mask. It was impossible to know even if the person was male or female.

"At least they're being COVID safe," Emily said.

"I don't think that's the reason for the mask," Jenny replied. "If you don't want to report this to the police, why not your solicitor. Don't you pay a stonking great retainer to a solicitor to solve problems for you? Do you ever call her? Maybe its time she earned her keep."

"Well, she is on retainer to give me advice about legals relating to my shares and such. She deals in financial and business law. I don't know she does much with people sneaking mean letters into the mailbox type things."

"Call her."

"You must be the world's bossiest nurse. I bet the junior nurses hated you at the hospital."

Jenny smiled, "Yes they did. Now call."

Emily called. Jessica listened to the story then asked, "Could it be your ex husband? I know it was a long time ago, but did you do at all well out of the divorce?"

"I got three kids, the clothes the four of us were standing up in, and his bills. He got everything else. Then he kept using my cards until I cancelled them and started over. I don't owe him."

Jessica made a slight humming noise while she thought.

"I don't want you to worry too much about this, but... I don't want you to ignore it either. Look this could be nothing. Rich people are sometimes targets for all kinds of nut jobs, but to be on the safe side, shoot me a copy of the security footage and a scan of the letter. Keep the original letter in a file, and don't handle it too much because it might have fingerprints on it. And keep a copy of the footage. Like I said, it could be nothing, but let's have a paper trail in case it turns out to be something."

# Chapter 2: Lunch

Emily carried the tray into her mother's sitting room.

"I thought we might have lunch together, if that's OK," she said.

Elsie had been watching the television. She turned her head to look at Emily, and gave a small smile. "What's your name, dear?" she asked.

Emily pulled the wheeled meal trolley over in front of her mother, and adjusted it to the right height. She put the lunch tray down in front of her mother, and then took her own plate and glass and sat them on the coffee table next to a second arm chair, where she sat.

"My name's Emily," she said, introducing herself to her mother for what seemed like the thousandth time.

"I've got a daughter named Emily," Elsie said, "she never comes to visit me though."

"I'm sorry to hear that. I'm sure she would come if she could."

"Oh corned beef and pickle sandwiches. These are my favourite" Elsie had changed the subject again, as she often did. She had trouble following a conversation.

"They're my mother's favourite, too," Emily said.

"My husband doesn't like them," Elsie said. "He doesn't like sandwiches. He says I have to cook him a proper lunch."

"Oh?" Emily said. "What's a proper lunch?"

"Meat and veggies. He wants meat and veggies for every meal. He's a busy man and I have to make sure his meals are ready when he wants them or he'll be angry. He teaches school, but he comes home for lunch, so I can cook it for him.

He won't eat sandwiches in the staff room like the other teachers."

From the snippets Emily heard about her father, she was glad she'd never met him. She suspected he and her ex-husband might have got along well.

"Oh well, he's not here, so we can have whatever we want for lunch," Emily said, conspiratorially.

"Oh yes, let's just have what we want. We won't tell Henry. Maybe we can have ice cream and jelly as well."

"I don't know if we've got any jelly made, but we can definitely have ice cream after we finish our sandwiches." Emily thought she should ask Carole to make jelly for the next day's lunch. She reflected sadly, that talking to her mother now was almost like talking to her daughters had been when they were toddlers. Even though Elsie was alive and physically fairly well, and sitting in front of her, Emily grieved the loss of the mother who had been so strong, so resilient, and whose mind had been so sharp. In days when it was rare for a woman to be a single mother, Elsie had managed to juggle work and raising Emily with a calm, efficient, strength.

They ate their sandwiches in silence for a while. Then Elsie asked: "What's your name again dear?"

"I'm Emily."

"Really? I have a daughter named Emily."

"You told me about her," Emily answered, sadly.

"Did I? She's very smart. She's got a degree. I never knew anyone with a degree before and she worked so hard for it. Even my husband only had a teaching certificate. They didn't need degrees back when he started. Emily was the first person I knew to get a degree. She's a very smart girl."

"You must be very proud of her."

"Oh I am very proud of her. But she never comes to see me. I think she's too busy. She's got a husband to look after now, and little children."

The little children were now thirty, twenty-seven and twenty-four. Two of them had children of their own. Elsie saw them all at least once each week, but never remembered them.

"That does sound like she's got her hands full," Emily said.

"I worry about her." Elsie whispered: "I think that awful husband beats her, just like Henry used to beat me."

She'd known, Emily realised. Back when she thought she was alone, when she thought no-one knew, her mother had known.

# Chapter 3: Jack

Emily was signing the form assigning her proxy votes for an annual general meeting of one of the companies she invested in.

"Some people who buy huge chunks of companies want to be more hands on," Jenny said.

"Some people don't know the limits of their expertise. I know mine," Emily said. "I pick good companies, with good environmental and social credentials, run by competent people. Then I trust those people to run the company without my incompetent interference. I'm an investor, nothing more."

"Fair enough. You don't want to go to the AGM, just to see it all happen?"

"Travel interstate, during a pandemic, with a compromised immune system, for a meeting that I'll get a full report on anyway? As my nurse, are you recommending that?"

"Not when you put it that way. It's just you never get out. You live in this tiny bubble. Your world is this house and your daughters and granddaughters. I worry about how healthy that is."

"I'm an introvert. I'm privileged to be able to live in my own little world. After everything that's happened in my life, I don't take that privilege lightly. I'm living the life I used to dream about. You don't need to worry about my mental health and isolation. I'm not lonely and I'm not missing out. My world is just as big as I want it to be, and it only includes people I want to be with."

The phone rang. It was Jack, Emily's ex-husband. Perhaps there were some people in her tiny world who she didn't want there. He wanted what he always wanted: to borrow money they both knew he would never repay.

13

"I want to take the grandkids to a theme park, but I'm a bit short of money this week," he said.

"Did you retire? Or are you still earning six figures a year?" she asked. Throughout their marriage, he'd always earned much more than her, but she'd always had to pay for all of the family's needs. His income was frittered away on frivolous things she didn't understand.

"You know I've never been good with money," he said. "I don't have anything. I just need enough to take the grandkids to a theme park."

Emily thought a moment. "I know you've always said you've never been good with money, but you've also never made any effort to learn to be responsible. You've always just wasted everything you got and counted on someone else, usually me, to bail you out. I shouldn't give you anything, but, since it's for the kids. Let's see. I've already given them annual passes to the parks, but there might be a park I missed. Theme park tickets are about a hundred dollars. For you and three kids, that's four hundred, I'll allow five hundred in case the price has gone up since I last took them. Once you're inside rides and shows are free, so you just need money for food and souvenirs, so you probably need about seven hundred. I'll be generous and give you a thousand. How's that?"

She waited for the inevitable whine. She knew it wasn't about the grandkids. It was never about the grandkids, just as it had never been about the kids. It was always about whatever unnecessary purchase he had decided he urgently needed.

"That's not enough. I need a hundred thousand."

"A hundred thousand? Which theme park do you need a hundred thousand dollars for? Are you taking three children out, or buying shares in the park?"

"I need transport to take them there!"

"You want me to buy you a new car."

"Well…"

"Don't you have a car?"

"Yes, but it's two years old."

Emily felt as if her head was exploding. She knew if Jenny took her blood pressure now, the reading would not be good.

"I'm not buying you a new car. I'll give you a thousand if you really are taking the grandkids out, but nothing more."

"But you can afford it!"

"I can afford it. So can you. You just choose to waste money and then complain you don't have money after you wasted it. That sounds like it's your problem, not mine."

"You used to be nicer than this."

"I used to be afraid of you. I'm not afraid any more. It's a thousand for the grandkids or nothing. Your choice. And don't leave me any more threatening letters. It's not going to work."

She wasn't sure he'd left the note, but his asking for money the same day seemed like too much of a coincidence. Clumsy demands for money, with lies about what he intended to use it for was his normal style, but the threat wasn't completely out of the realm of possibility.

"What threatening letter?"

"The one you left in my letterbox, calling me a bitch, and demanding an unspecified amount of money 'or else', which I have to say is the most insipid threat ever. 'Or else' what? You're going to kick and scream? You're going to hold your breath until you turn blue. You're going on a hunger strike? You're going to try to break into my very secure house to assault me. You've got to do better than that. If you're going to extort me for money tell me how much and what you'll do if I don't pay."

"I didn't sent you any threatening letter. I wouldn't do that. I'm not that kind of person."

"I was married to you for a decade. I know you're absolutely that kind of person, whatever you like to think about yourself. You're cheap and selfish and nasty, and you use people. I get that letter first thing this morning, and this afternoon, you call and name your price. You're not as subtle as you think."

"I don't know anything about a letter. I just called because I thought it would be nice to take our grandchildren to a theme park. But you don't care about our grandchildren. You're only thinking about yourself like you always do. You're a selfish, horrible person.You've got all that money and you don't share it or spend it on anyone. You just hoard it."

"You mean I don't give it all to you. That doesn't make me selfish. It just means I've learned a lot over the years. If I gave you everything I have, you'd waste it and be broke in no time anyway. Do you want the thousand dollars or not?"

"Of course I want it. That's the least you can do."

"The least I can do is nothing, which is what I ought to do. OK. I'll do the bank transfer now. Enjoy the day out. Please try not to put the girls on wild rides straight after filling them up with greasy junk food."

She pressed the "end call" button before he could say any more.

Was he telling the truth?  Did he not have anything to do with the note?

With the tension headache building, Emily wrote a note detailing the conversation, and added it to the file with the original threatening note. Maybe the conversation was evidence her ex-husband was behind the threat. Maybe it just proved he was a jerk, something she'd already known.

# Chapter 4: Fatigue

Emily took a deep breath. The headache was overwhelming. The stress of the day was taking its toll on her body.

Lupus fatigue hit with full force. All of her muscles felt weak. A fuzzy feeling not quite like pins and needles overcame her whole body. Her stomach turned to jelly, wobbling, building up to release everything. She was both hot and cold. Overloaded nerves sent contradictory messages to her brain. Clammy perspiration covered her entire body. Her hair was soaked with sweat and too hot for her head, yet she was shivering with cold. Her vision lost some of its focus, as her overworked brain stopped bothering to fully interpret the signals from her eyes. She had that too familiar feeling of unreality, that she was there and yet not there. The world was fog and she was mist lost in it.

"I'm out of spoons," she said.[1] "I need to go lie down."

Emily put both hands flat on her desk, on either side of the laptop computer. She pushed against the table to stand up, wavered for a minute, and collapsed back into her office chair.

"Stay there," Jenny said. "I'll get the wheelchair."

Logically, it would only have taken Jenny a couple of minutes to get the wheelchair from Elsie's suite, but Emily's deep state of fatigue, it could have been seconds or it could have been years.

---

[1] "Spoons" is a common metaphor used by people with chronic illness to talk about the level of energy or fatigue they feel. It comes from Christine Miserandino's *Spoon Theory* which can be found in full at https://butyoudontlooksick.com/articles/written-by-christine/the-spoon-theory/.

"OK, arms around my neck," Jenny said. "We transfer on the count of three. One. Two. Three, up… and down."

Emily cooperated as much as she was able.

Jenny picked up Emily's unresponding feet and put them on the wheelchair's foot rests. She wheeled Emily to her bedroom, and helped transfer her to the bed.

"How's your pain, on a scale of one to ten?" Jenny asked.

Emily heard the feint voice from a long way away. "Not bad," she answered slowly. "Maybe a six or seven."

"You know, people who don't have chronic pain consider a six or seven to be quite bad."

"Lucky them," Emily answered weakly.

Jenny went to a small ornate desk beside Emily's matching ornate dressing table. On top of the desk was Emily's weekly pills, in a sorting box, sorted by day and time, each day in its own box in the larger frame. She picked up the day's box, then pulled out the desk's drawer and pulled out three boxes of medications in their original packaging. She opened the "evening" section of the pill sorter box, and added one of each of the tablets she'd taken from the drawer, and carried it to Emily's bedside.

"Take your night time pills now, so you don't have to wake up again later. I've added an anti-diarrhoea tablet so your tummy doesn't let you down again, some temazipam to help you sleep and some oxycodone to block the pain for a few hours.

"It's only four o'clock," Emily tried to argue. Her voice was as weak as her body.

"Your body's done for the day whatever your brain might want," Jenny said. "Although, I suspect your brain doesn't really want to keep going either. It's just your stubborn, independent streak that wants to stay awake."

19

She handed the pills, and the water bottle Emily kept on a bedside table to her patient. Emily took the pills, and Jenny put the pill box back in the sorter tray, closed the curtains to cut down the afternoon light, wished Emily a good night and left the room.

Emily was troubled with strange dreams of a menacing shadow figure, undefined threats, of a secret that needed to be discovered, a mystery with no clues.

Occasionally the dreams changed to Jack wheedling and whining, accusing and gaslighting, threatening and menacing.

Then back her mind went to the mysterious shadow figure, an unknown person who thought she knew what they wanted.

Where they the same? Her troubled mind went from one to the other in her sleep, unable to come to a resolution.

# Chapter 5: Rock

It was the weekend. Jenny and Carole were both on days off. Emily's youngest daughter Kym was staying with her, to help care for Elsie. Ever since Elsie had come to live with Emily, Emily's daughters had taken turns to stay for the weekend. Then, on Sunday, the whole family would come for a barbecue together.

Emily and Kym were changing sheets on Elsie's bed.

"I didn't know adult nappies could leak so badly," Kym said. "And Jenny always says she could look after Grandma in a couple of half hour visits a day."

"I think Jenny overstates her efficiency a little," Emily said, "Although she's a good nurse and I can't fault her work."

Emily stretched her aching back. "I wonder if it's time to hire a weekend nurse as well," she said. "Jenny has the flat, which was probably servants' quarters when this place was built, but a weekend nurse could stay in one of the guest rooms. It's really only Christmas when you girls are all here that the guest rooms get used."

Kym finished making the bed. "You know we're all happy to help, but having a nurse as well would probably be useful. I heard Dad's been hitting you up for money again," she said.

"Oh you heard?"

"Yeah, he called both Alannah and Jody and complained he wanted to take their kids to a theme park but you were being mean and wouldn't give him the money he needed. They both told him you'd already given them and the kids annual passes to all of the Gold Coast parks. Jody offered him fifty for petrol."

"I gave him a thousand, in case he actually was going to take the kids out."

"A thousand? And he's still complaining! When they already have tickets? What did he expect?"

"He wanted a hundred thousand."

"For a trip to a theme park - was he going to one overseas?"

"For a new car. Apparently he could only take them in a new car."

"He got a new car not long ago."

"Two years ago, apparently."

They looked at each other and laughed.

"Anyway, Alannah's coming to help you with Grandma next weekend, and Jody and I are taking the kids to Dreamworld on Saturday. I haven't seen the kids since Easter, so it will be good to see them, hype them up on sugar and walk away. Being an aunt's great, all the fun and no responsibility."

They were interrupted by the sound of glass shattering. Following the sound, Kym ran and Emily walked to the entry hall. One of large windows beside the front door was smashed. Among the shards of broken glass, on the marble tiled floor, was a rock, with a piece of paper wrapped around it and tied with string.

"Well, that's an uncivilised way to send a message. Yesterday's nasty note was just dropped in the letter box. This seems much more unfriendly," Emily said.

"What nasty note?"

"An anonymous person called me a bitch and claimed I owed them an unspecified amount of money. I called Jessica Flowers. She told me to keep it in case the issue escalated and we needed to call the police."

Kym carefully stepped through the broken glass, and removed the note from the rock. "I'd say this is an escalation. Maybe you should call Jessica again," she said.

She handed the note to Emily. Again in untidy capitals, it said, "YOU GOT EVERYTHING. I GOT NOTHING. GIVE ME MY SHARE OR DIE!"

"They still don't say who they are, or how much they want, or why they think I owe them. I'm sure a bit more clarity would help. Yes, I'll make the call," Emily said.

She called Jessica on her private after-hours line. Jessica advised her to avoid touching anything they hadn't already handled, and wait for her to call back.

Ten minutes later, Jessica called back and advised that a police officer, Detective Carstairs was on the way to see them.

Detective Sergeant Angie Carstairs arrived with Detective Constable Eric Morley and a team of forensic technicians.

They took both notes, the video file from the first note, and video of possibly the same person in a hoodie hurling the rock over the front fence and through the window.

"That's actually quite a good throw," Emily said, watching the playback. "Maybe they play cricket or something."

Emily answered the expected questions. No, she didn't owe anyone any money. The only person who had asked her for money was Jack. No, she couldn't think of anyone who would do this.

The police officers took notes. The forensics people took photos and made measurements. Then they took the rock and string.

Eventually Detective Carstairs gave Emily her business card and asked her to call if anything more were to happen. She wrote her after hours number on the back of the card, and promised police would have an increased presence in the area, at least for a while.

Kym had gone to sit with Elsie. Emily swept up the glass, and called a glazier.

# Chapter 6: Watercolour

Kym, a professional artist, had brought watercolours and paper to paint with Elsie.

When Emily had cleaned up the broken window glass, she'd found them at the dining room table, with a canvas drop sheet over the table and art supplies spread out.

"Do you want to paint with us, Mum?" Kym asked.

Emily sat down at the table, and Kym handed her a sheet of paper. She looked over at Kym's work. "Children's book?" she asked.

"Yeah. Just recently got it. The author has a cute story. I hope I'm doing it justice.' She was adding the finishing touches to a purple elephant holding a bunch of roses in its trunk.

"It's adorable. Kids will love it." Emily said.

"What did the police say after I came back to Grandma?" Kym asked.

"The police?" Elsie responded. "Oh they were looking for Henry."

"We meant the police who were here. They were trying to find out who threw the rock through the window."

"Oh that was the girl's father," Elsie said.

"What? What girl's father threw the rock."

"Oh yes, he threw rocks through the windows and yelled for Henry to go out and face him. Henry didn't go out of course. Henry said the man was dumb and drunk and just to ignore him. He said we'd just wait for the man to sober up and go away."

"And did he sober up and go away?" Kym asked.

"Well he went away when the police came. I think the neighbours called. He must have sobered up eventually. People usually do, don't they?"

"Why was he throwing rocks and yelling? Had Henry done something to make the man angry?" Emily asked. Like her daughter, she was intrigued by this snippet of family history.

"Because he was the girl's father. You can't go around treating girls like that and think their fathers won't get angry."

"Treating girls like what? Was Henry having an affair?"

"What's your name, dear?" Elsie asked.

"I'm Emily, and this is my daughter Kym."

"How strange! My daughter's Emily, and her little baby's named Kym."

"Yes, total coincidence," Kym answered. "Tell us more about Henry and the girl."

"Henry? Oh Henry's gone now. He went away."

"Do you know where he went?" Emily asked.

"Who are you, dear?" Elsie asked.

"I think you might be getting tired," Emily said.

"Oh yes, I am very tired," Elsie said.

"Let's get you to bed then," Kym said. Kym helped Elsie from the dining chair to a wheelchair, and wheeled her to her bedroom, then carefully helped her to bed.

Emily made coffee for herself and Kym.

"I wonder if your father was having an affair," Kym said. "Maybe that's why he disappeared. He went off with this girl Grandma was talking about."

"I guess it's possible," Emily said. "I mean, Mum never told me any reason why he left. He was never there during my childhood, and Mum always just said he'd gone away. I don't even know if he left before I was born, or when I was a baby. He left early enough, that I don't remember him at all. Mum didn't even keep pictures of him. I don't know what he looked like."

"I wonder if she actually knew where he was. If he'd had an affair and gone off with the other woman."

"She never said so if she did know. This, today, is the most she's ever said about him."

"Mum, you look tired. You should go for a nap while Grandma's asleep."

"The glazier's coming."

"I'll take care of the glazier. I mean, it's pretty obvious what the job is, and he can either send you a bill, or I can pay him. You get some rest, while Grandma's asleep."

"It seems so selfish, having a nap and leaving you to deal with things."

"Selfish? You?"

"Your father says I am."

"When you won that money, the first thing you did was give ten million each to Alannah, Jody and me, and told us to follow our dreams. Then you said if our dreams cost more than that to come back for more. You give half your investment income away to charity. You aren't well enough to look after Grandma, but you do, because she told you she would never want to go to a nursing home. You pay your staff probably twice what they'd be paid anywhere else. You pay for Alannah's and Jody's kids' education, and their out of school activities. You give in to Dad over and over and pay for far too much of his lifestyle. Back when we were kids, and we were broke, you always made sure we had what we needed, even though you went without so much. I know you missed meals, but you made sure we didn't. No Mum, you aren't selfish. You're the lest selfish person I know. Now go and get some rest. I'll deal with the glazier, and I'll cook dinner."

Emily went for a nap, and dreamed once more of a faceless lurking figure who wanted something from her.

# Chapter 7: Kid

Emily updated Jenny on the weekend's events over morning coffee. Carole listened in while she cleaned the kitchen.

"I'm glad the police are taking it seriously," Carole said.

"The detective said throwing a rock through a window is destruction of property, so that's an actual offence they could act on, and the "or die" in the second note is a definite threat. She said it would have been iffy about whether the first note was any kind of criminal offence. This second note, with the rock, that's enough for them to investigate. Obviously, though, they can only do something about it, if they can find the person who threw it."

"And this is why men get away with intimidating women so often," Jenny said. "Vague threats aren't enough for police to bother. They have to actually say they're going to kill you, in a way that convinces the police they're serious."

"Honestly, I didn't think the first note was worth any bother, either," Emily said. "And this person still hasn't explained what they think I owe them. It seems as if they think I know. I wish they'd just spell it out. As it is, I feel like I'm being threatened by shadows."

They were interrupted by the sound of male voices yelling in front of the house.

All three women ran to the front door to see Josh, the gardener, holding a teenaged boy by the hood of his hoodie. The teenager was struggling, trying to twist his way out of Josh's grip. Josh was holding on tight.

"This kid was about to lob a rock though the window," he said.

"Well thanks for preventing that, Josh," Emily answered. "I had to replace a window on Saturday, and don't want to replace another one today." To the kid she said, "Why not just give me the note now, instead of getting yourself in more trouble with the police?"

"Police?" the kid seemed panicked.

"You can't go giving people death threats and smashing windows without the police taking an interest. Surely you're old enough to know that," Emily said.

"Death threats? No. He just said I had to deliver messages to his sister to make her give him his share of his inheritance. He said his sister stole it from him."

"So you didn't write this?" Emily asked, taking the note and reading it out. Again it was in untidy capitals. It said, "GIVE ME WHAT'S MINE OR I WILL KILL YOU."

"What? No!" the kid said. "He just told me to deliver that first note and then when he didn't get his money he gave me notes tied to rocks and told me to throw them through the window."

"Who is he?"

"You should know. He's your brother."

"What brother? I don't have a brother. I was an only child. What makes you think he's my brother?" Emily said. "I don't know who this person is, or what money he thinks I owe him. I haven't collected any inheritance, mine or anyone else's."

"He said he was your brother."

"Well, he's not."

"But that's what he told me."

"And what made you think he was telling the truth?"

"Why wouldn't he?"

"Could it possibly be because he was manipulating you into delivering death threats to a stranger?

"You mean he lied to me? I believed him, but he lied to me?"

"Yes. So who is he?"

"I don't know. He contacted me on the internet. He called himself 'U. N. Known'. He put the notes and instructions and money to pay me in my mailbox."

Emily sighed. "Well, come in now, we'll get you a coffee and I'll call the police. Let's see if we can get you out of this problem U. N. Known got you into."

Inside, the kid sat at the dining table, with Josh standing behind him, watching in case he tried to run. Jenny and Carole sat opposite. Emily, sitting at the head of the table, called the number on Detective Sergeant Carstairs' card and told the story.

"The police are on their way. After they've been, I'm going to call my solicitor. I need to tell her what is happening, but I will also get her to arrange someone to represent you if the police arrest you."

"I can't afford a solicitor," the kid said. He sounded quiet, subdued, and he avoided looking directly at Emily.

"I can. How about you tell me your name, so I know who I'm hiring a solicitor for."

The kid was gave his name as Jacob Henderson, known as Jake. He asked, "Why would you hire a solicitor for me?"

"Because I don't think you did this on your own. I don't think you were acting maliciously. I think you were tricked, used by someone else, and I think you believed them, because you don't have the life experience to know you were being manipulated. They deserve to be punished. You just need to learn to be careful who you trust."

Detectives Carstairs and Morley arrived. They listened to the story, and got statements from everyone, particularly Jake. Then they took the kid, the rock, the note, and the string that held the rock and note together.

Emily called Jessica, and told her all that had happened. She asked if Jessica could organise someone to represent the kid.

"You seriously want to pay for a solicitor for someone who delivered death threats to you and smashed your window?" Jessica asked.

"He's just a kid," Emily said. "And he's a kid naïve enough to just believe a stranger on the internet. Apart from that, the clothes he was wearing today were exactly the same as the clothes he wore when he delivered both previous notes. Not similar, the same. That tells me he doesn't have much. So, yes, I'll pay for his representation. And I'd like to know about his living situation. He said U. N. Known had put everything in the letter box for him, so he does have a roof over his head, but if he didn't have anyone tell him this wasn't a good idea, either his parents don't care, or something is wrong. Maybe he or his family need help. I raised kids with next to nothing, I know how hard it is."

"I will get someone from our criminal law department to represent him. I'll have them ask about his living situation, but he'll have to give permission for the information to be passed on to you."

"Fair enough. The kid's already been manipulated and betrayed. I'm not going to make it worse by stomping over his rights," Emily said.

After ending the call, Emily looked around at Jenny and Carole. "So what's next?" she asked.

"Lunch, I think," Carole answered. "Would you like to eat in the dining room or shall I put together a tray for you to take to your mother's sitting room?"

"Let's bring Mum out to the dining room, and we can all eat together. Perhaps we could invite Josh to join us."

Carole did not look entirely happy. She preferred to take lunch out to Josh, so he didn't track dirt into the house, but she nodded.

# Chapter 8: Henry

Emily sat beside her mother at the table. She noticed Carole had put a towel on a seat for Josh to sit on. Dining chairs so valuable they had to be protected from dirty people suddenly struck her as absurd. She could remember her three kids running in from outside, having to be nagged to even wash their hands and faces before eating, and then coming to the table thoroughly dishevelled and dirty.

"Hello," have you eaten here before?" Elsie said

"Yes, I have. Quite often, in fact," Emily answered. "The cook here is very talented."

"What's your name, dear?"

"I'm Emily."

"I have a daughter named Emily!"

"I think you've told me about her before."

"She doesn't come to visit me though."

"I'm sorry about that. Have you met everyone else?"

Emily introduced the people Elsie saw five days per week.

When the introductions got to Josh, Elsie asked: "Is this your young man?"

"No, Josh is the gardener. He grows those amazing roses, the ones we put in the vase in your room."

"Roses. Roses always make me think of my husband, Henry."

"That's nice," Emily said. "Did he grow roses?"

"Oh no, not him. Henry never grew anything. He wouldn't let me grow a garden. I grew roses after he left."

"Oh, I see." Emily did not see.

The conversation turned to the events of the past few days, the notes, the threats, the arrest of Jacob Henderson.

"I can't believe he, whoever he is, involved a kid."

"No," Elsie said. "He shouldn't have involved the kid. Henry should have known better."

"Henry? He involved a kid in something?" Emily asked.

"She was his student. He shouldn't have done it."

Everyone was looking at Elsie.

"Done what?" Emily asked.

"He got her pregnant, dear,"Elsie said.

"But didn't you tell me he taught primary school? He taught little children."

"She was a child. A child had a child. Henry shouldn't have done that."

"No," Jenny said. "He absolutely should not."

"What happened to the child?" Emily asked.

"What child, dear?" Elsie asked.

"Henry's child."

"Emily? I think she's gone outside to play. I should go and check on her."

"It's all right, we'll check on her," Emily said.

Everyone around the table seemed to be in shocked silence. This was a revelation no-one expected.

Emily was, once again, glad she had not known her father.

"What's you're name again, dear," Elsie asked.

"I'm Emily, and these are my friends," Emily said.

"Oh how nice! My daughter's name is Emily. She doesn't visit me though, I think she might be too busy."

Emily put her elbows on the table, and put her face in her hands. She didn't think she could cope with any more.

Josh spoke up, "Hey Mrs Clark, would you like to come out to the garden with me? I could show you the roses?"

"Oh yes," Elsie said. "Do you know roses always remind me of my husband, Henry."

"Really? Josh said, "Well, we've got some lovely ones in the garden here. The Dark Desires are blooming nicely now, and there's a beautiful Blue Moon but just starting to open. Then there's the Perfume Passion as well, they're really looking and smelling great at the moment."

He wheeled the elderly woman's wheelchair out of the back door.

Carole quietly started to clear away dishes.

Jenny put a hand gently on Emily's shoulder.

"It all just gets worse and worse," Emily said.

"Your mother never told you before?"

"No. She's kept that a secret all this time. The other day she was telling Kym and me about a girl's father coming yelling for Henry. I didn't think 'girl' meant primary school girl. She had to be twelve or younger. My father was a monster."

"And yet you turned out to be so kind you'd provide a lawyer for a kid who delivered death threats to you. You can't change the past or who he was."

"If he had a child, somewhere out there I could have a sister or brother. This person who sent Jacob really could be a sibling I didn't know about."

"Even if they are, any remotely sane person would have sent you a letter, or phoned or contacted you on social media, and introduced themselves."

"So they're crazy? You don't think they might actually believe I knew whatever it is they were talking about? I don't think that makes it any better."

"Even if they did think you knew, they should have gone about it differently."

"I guess I should tell the police about this." Emily said. "I think I'll call Jessica as well."

Josh wheeled Elsie back in from the yard.

"This young man's a gardener," Elsie informed them. "He grows the most wonderful roses. You really should see them."

"We've seen them," Emily said. "And you're right, they are perfect. Josh is an incredibly good gardener."

"Who is Josh, dear?" Elsie asked, "and what's your name?"

# Chapter 9: Detectives?

Emily called Detective Carstairs first, and explained what Elsie had said.

"We'll look into that," the detective said, "and we're having a word with your ex-husband as well. The kid's co-operating, but he doesn't seem to know anything more than he already told you. We've traced the original contact he had back to a computer at the local library, and the only fingerprints on the notes apart from yours are his. The person pulling his strings was smart enough to wear gloves, apparently."

Emily thanked her, and then called Jessica.

"Do you have your own private detectives there?" she asked.

"Private detectives? You mean like fictional lawyers on American tv shows have on staff? No. We don't have any of those. Why do you ask?"

"I guess that was asking too much. I want to know where my father went after he left my mother, and what happened to his child. Maybe who the child was. I know the police are going to try to find all of that out, but I was hoping you might have the resources to find out faster?"

"Well I don't have a detective, but I have a clerk who is good at searching public records, things like birth, deaths, marriages, property transfers, and electoral rolls. Let's see what she can find out."

"I know it might not lead anywhere."

"But it could lead somewhere, and now you need to know. I'll do what I can."

"And what about the kid? Jacob Henderson? Was he willing to have you tell me his story?"

"Yes, and it is a sad story. When you said you didn't think he had anyone, you were pretty close. Mum's in behind bars, serious drug offences. She's not getting out in the foreseeable future. Dad's not in the picture, hasn't been as long as he can remember. He's in the foster care system, been kicked from one carer to another over and over. He actually told his foster parents about U. N. Known."

"And they didn't tell him it was a bad idea, and probably illegal?"

"He told them U. N. Known had offered him two hundred dollars for each message he delivered. They encouraged him and took the money from him. He doesn't have anything of his own and shares a room with two other foster kids."

"I want to help him," Emily said.

"You're providing him a solicitor. When you get our bill this month you might decide you've helped him more than enough. You aren't responsible for him."

"But the adults who are responsible for him have let him down. What do you think would have happened to me if my mother had been like the adults in his life? What would have happened to my kids if I had been like them? Surely someone should do something. I'm someone with the resources. Can I pay his expenses? Get him an education?"

"If you give him money outright, I suspect it will go the same way as the money U. N. Known paid him."

"Can we bypass the foster parents somehow?"

"I could set up a trust, whereby the trust pays expenses that are invoiced to it, or reimburses on presentation of receipts. It's not foolproof. They could submit invoices for things they then sell instead of giving it to the kid."

"Would that be legal?"

"Submitting expenses, and then selling the item? No that wouldn't be legal. That would be fraud, but people do it. People who would let a kid under their care deliver death threats, just so they can get money, probably wouldn't be above a bit of mild fraud. We'd also have to negotiate with the Family Services Department, since he's in care. They might object to one kid in care getting something others didn't."

"I guess that's fair enough. I know I can't help every kid in trouble, but there's something about this one. I suppose because he's the one who turned up on my doorstep. And because, you said his father left him, like my father left me. Can you contact the Department, see if it's doable, and if so start whatever paperwork needs to be done to establish the trust."

"You'll need to appoint trustees. This firm could do that, but there will be a cost, and you'll have to decide whether you want that cost to come out of the trust or if you'll pay it directly. And you'll have to think about how much you want to give him, and what happens when he ages out. When he's an adult does he get whatever money's left, or does it go back to you. That kind of thing. It's a lot to consider, so you're going to need to think about it if you really want to go ahead. It might be easier to just give the money to a charity for disadvantaged kids."

"It might be easier, but I still want to help this particular kid. So if you can look into it, I'd appreciate that. Can you email me all those questions you wanted me to think about? My thinker is all thunk out at the moment."

# Chapter 10: Settlement

Emily was really not ready for another call from Jack, but calls from Jack usually came when she wasn't ready for them. It was probably because she was never really ready for them.

Jack was angry. When was he not angry?

"Why did you tell the police I was threatening you and trying to get money from you?"

"I didn't tell them you were. Someone is threatening me and trying to extort money from me. The first time, as soon as I'd heard from them, I heard from you as well. So the police are investigating who might want money from me, and who would threaten to kill me to get it."

"Well, I never threatened you."

"I didn't tell them you did. I did tell them I heard from you after I got the first message, and, like the person who sent the message, you wanted money from me."

"You've got all that money and you keep it to yourself, of course I'm going to ask for money from you. It's not fair that you don't share it with me."

Emily sighed, "That's the wonder of divorce. You don't get what's mine now. And if you weren't behind the threats and the extortion attempts, I'm sure the police will work that out and stop bothering you. If you're having trouble understanding why they have to investigate, one of your daughters was here when one of the threats was thrown on a rock through the window. Don't worry, Kym wasn't hurt. I'm sure you were just about to ask about her welfare."

"Maybe you should just give them the money they're looking for. Then none of the girls would be in danger. But you're too selfish to do that. You would risk the girls' safety so you can keep all your money. That's just the kind of person you are. It's all about you, and making sure you've got everything you want."

"That's not in the least true. It never has been. So what is this call about? Are you just wanting to rant about police doing their job? Is there something else? You want me to buy a luxury car or a yacht or something stupid for you? You spent all your money and need someone to pay your bills? You've found another way to use the kids or grandkids as a means of trying to get money out of me? What is it? Just spit it out, because I've already had pretty much all I can take today!"

"I was talking to Geoff at work about this whole police thing, and you accusing me of trying to get money from you."

"Oh and what brilliant, enlightened, thing did Geoff have to say about the matter? Leave it to the police to work out? Answer questions honestly and you won't have a problem? Stop demanding money so you don't look suspicious? What?"

"Well he said, I should already have half your money."

"On really? I can't wait for the justification for this. Is it going to be a long story? Should I get popcorn?"

"He said when you get divorced you each get half the money. So I should have half your money."

"Did you happen to mention to him that when we got divorced, you took all the money we had between us? That I did not, in fact, have any money then? That the kids and I had nothing, and spent years struggling just for the basics of survival?"

"He said women hide money all the time in divorces, and you were probably rich all along. He said you were manipulating me, trying to make me think I got my share, but you were really hiding money. He said there's all kinds of tricks for hiding money, and someone rich like you would know all of them."

"You know I got my money from a lotto win, years after we were divorced. You know that. I know you know that because that's when I gave the girls their money, and then you turned up, asking for money. You can't backdate it. If you took it to a court, they'd laugh at you."

"I trust Geoff. He's a good bloke, and he's really smart. He thinks I should get a lawyer and take you to court."

"Well, you do that. Seriously. And when we pull out all the records and bank statements from the time, and all the bills you left me with, the court will probably decide you owe me money. Geoff is right about one thing: we should have gone to court for a property settlement, even with the little we had. It's my fault we didn't. I was just so desperate to be free of you, I didn't care what it cost. That meant the kids and I had to scrounge and struggle, and it was so much harder than it should have been, especially since you continued running up debts in my name, until I cancelled everything you had access to. So sure, let's go to court. I'll give you my solicitor's contact details and your solicitor can call her. In the meantime, I'll grab the file with all the bank statements and everything, because, as you know, I never throw out anything." Emily was shaking with both fatigue and anger. How dare this pathetic excuse for a human being try to gaslight her like this?

"Geoff says I'll definitely win. So, maybe I will do it, and you can pay me everything you owe me."

"Well Geoff is clearly not a divorce lawyer, and is also either not very smart, or unclear on the real situation. Since he's apparently male, you will listen to what he says instead of anything I might say, so you do whatever you think you need to. You do realise, that carrying on about this is exactly the kind of thing that makes the police consider you a suspect? You realise, I have to tell them about this conversation, because they want to know if anyone is asking me for money."

"Only because you lie to them and tell them I'm a suspect. I bet it's all a lie, that no-one threatened you and this is all to get me in trouble. You're just trying to get attention."

"Ah yes, I'm threatened, and it's about you. I wondered when that would happen. No I wouldn't lie to get you in trouble. I have much better things to do than dealing with you. The only time I even think about you is when you call, because you really don't matter to me at all. You're just a part of my history, and the girls are the only part of that that I don't regret."

"I don't think about you either."

"That's why you call me twice a week. Why don't you get on with your life? Find someone else to make miserable? Get a hobby? Make friends with people who don't set you up to do and say stupid things?"

Jack hung up.

Emily was relieved the call was over.

After this call, she was almost certain Jack was not U. N. Known. He didn't have the brains for it, and he would have felt compelled to tell her or the girls what he was doing and whose idea it was. He always called someone to tell them whatever silly thing his workmates had suggested he do. He called everyone and told them everything.

Emily took a deep breath, and let it out slowly. She was utterly exhausted. It was going to be another day she went to bed for the night in the mid afternoon.

Before she could do that, she called Jessica, in case Jack found a solicitor stupid, or poorly informed, enough to take his case.

# Chapter 11: Records

Emily's call to Jessica the previous afternoon had been only a couple of minutes to give some forewarning about Jack's plan to seek out a financial settlement.

After that, she'd called Jenny to help her get to bed for the rest her brain and body desperately needed.

This morning, she had a clear head again, when Jessica called her.

Jessica's first piece of information was that Jack, had indeed called her. She had explained to him exactly what Emily had, that any court settlement would be based on the assets of the marriage at the time it ended, and it was very likely Jack would owe her money. Jack had insisted he was going to court anyway, then asked Jessica how to do that. As politely as she could, Jessica had explained she represented Emily, not him, and he either had to hire a solicitor of his own, or work it out.

"He seriously wanted you to give him legal advice, to sue me? I suppose he would have wanted me to pay for that, too," Emily was once more amazed she'd not only married this man, but also stuck with him so long. She had been so young and naive back then, and no idea what a healthy marriage looked like.

"He seriously did. He was angry. Really angry. I think he might go through with this. Can you get your bank to provide records from that time? We might possibly need them. And any records of house, vehicle ownership, that type of thing?"

"I can do better than that," Emily answered. "I never throw away legal or financial documents. I can give you the statements on the joint account right up to the time he cancelled my access, the details of setting up a new account for my wages to go into, the accounts he kept charging things to, that were in my name, the rental agreement that shows we didn't own the house, and even the details of the car, which he kept."

"Can you scan all of that and email it to me?" Jessica said. "If he gets a solicitor, I can probably use that to prove he doesn't have a case, and maybe save going to court."

"Of course," Emily said.

"I mean, if you do want to go to court, that's fine, we can. You can get back your share of the marital assets, or at least your share of the value."

"No, I don't need it, and if the threat is enough to get him to back off, that would be fine. Given everything else, I don't need the extra stress. Honestly, it would just mean increasing the amount he owes me, that he's never going to repay."

"Well, apart from the Jack update, I have to tell you what my clerk found. I'm sad to say, it is as bad as it seemed from what your mother said."

Emily sighed. "Tell me the worst. Just how bad was my father?"

"First we have records of birth from fifty-five years ago. Henry Clark is listed as father on two birth records, yours in March, and in September Henry Clark is listed as father of a Henry Clark Henderson, child of Kerry Henderson, aged twelve."

"Twelve? Oh no. Did my father go to jail for this? Is that where he was through my childhood? And what happened to the baby?"

"The only court records my clerk could find for your father was a warrant issued for his arrest, no sign he was actually brought before the court, so presumably he wasn't caught. The electoral roll still has his address as your childhood home, so he's never updated it. Nothing in public records indicates he even still exists.  Police can access some things we can't, so perhaps they know more."

Jessica allowed a moment for Emily to absorb that information. Then she continued: "As for the child, Henry Clark Henderson appears in records again fifteen years ago when he was father of a child, Jacob Clark Henderson."

"Jacob Henderson? Jake? The kid who delivered the messages?"

"That Jacob Henderson, yes. If Henry Clark Henderson is U. N. Known, he's using his own son to deliver his messages. That's really going to put him in the running for father of the year."

"Henry Clark Henderson, is my half brother, and maybe he used his own son to try to extort money from me. Maybe he thought I knew he existed.  Maybe he thought I inherited something, presumably from my, our, father? I know I asked for this information.  Now I don't know what I'm going to do with it. I mean, there's a lot of maybes there, but the actual known part is I have a half brother I never knew about."

"I can make a suggestion?  Give me permission to pass all of this along to the police."

"Of course. OK so what we know now is: Jack is probably not U. N. Known, but a half-brother, with the same first name as my absent father, probably is. Of course, it could also be that my father is manipulating both his son and grandson, since we don't know where he is. Or is that stretching it too far? Am I overthinking now?"

"We haven't found any death record for your father, but we can search again, if that helps eliminate one potential suspect," Jessica said. "You're right, if he is alive, he could be behind everything.  He might have told his son you inherited from a grandparent or great-grandparent or anyone. He could be pulling strings. At the moment, all we know about him is that he's the kind of man who would take advantage of a child entrusted to his care."

"And Jake, who is just a kid, is dragged into all of this. Well he's not just some kid now, he's apparently my nephew. I have to help him. Is there any way to try to get custody or guardianship or something? Can you please check into that? Of course, get the solicitor you have representing him ask if that's something he would want. I don't want to force that on him, but he does need a break."

"In the middle of your crazy ex suing you for money you don't owe, and possibly your half-brother, maybe with your father as well, trying to extort you, you still want to help this kid?"

"Yeah. Because he's a kid. Because he might have got involved, but he's not responsible for this. Because if I'd known I had a half-brother and a nephew, I'd probably have done something to support them anyway."

"I'll see what the options are," Jessica said. "But do not give money to U. N. Known. Giving in to this will only cause serious problems. I'm going to call Detective Carstairs, and give her the information we've found. Don't you do anything more, about any of this until you speak to me again."

# Chapter 12: Sunday Lunch

After a quiet couple of days, Emily was happy to have her daughters and their families come for a barbecue lunch.

Emily's oldest daughter Alannah, with her husband Steve, were at the barbecue, cooking steaks. Jody, Kym, Elsie and Emily were sitting nearby, talking, while the children ran around the garden, playing.

Emily filled her daughters in on all she'd learned from Jessica, about her having a half-brother, and that Jake, the boy who had delivered the threats, had been his son.

"Have there been any more threats since the police picked up Jake?" Jody asked.

"No," Emily answered, "thankfully. Maybe U. N. Known, whether or not he is Henry Henderson, has given up now that Jake isn't around to be manipulated by him."

"I hope so," Kym said. "That rock incident was scary. It's freaky that the boy who threw it is our cousin and none of us knew. Poor kid."

"Has anyone heard from Dad?" Jody asked.

"More than I wanted to," Emily said.

"About how he wanted to take the kids to a theme park, but Mum only gave him a thousand dollars, so he couldn't?" Kym answered. "Yeah, I heard."

"You gave him a thousand dollars?" Alannah asked. "And that wasn't enough? The kids all have annual passes to all the parks. What did he need a thousand dollars for, and why wasn't it enough?"

"He wanted enough to buy a new car," Kym answered. "But no, the latest is he called me yesterday and told me he's going to get half Mum's money."

"How's he going to do that?" Jody asked.

"He's suing me for a divorce settlement, or says he's going to," Emily said. "He thinks he's going to get rich."

"But doesn't that only apply to what you had at the time of the divorce?" Jody asked.

Emily sighed. "I did try to tell him that. Jessica Flowers tried to tell him that. He thinks I had money all along and was somehow hiding it from him. One of his workmates told him I would have done that, that rich people hide money in divorces."

"I wish you'd had money all along," Alannah said. "We could have done with it."

"Oh we really could have," Kym said. "Anyway, he's convinced he's getting a court to make Mum give him half her money."

"Won't he end up having to pay Mum?" Jody asked, "he got the house and everything.

"Well, the house was rented, but he did get everything we did own. So, he's not getting anything in any settlement. Did he eventually take the kids for a day out?" Emily said.

"Of course not," Alannah said. "I don't know why you give him money at all. He never uses it for what he says he's going to."

"I keep hoping he really does plan to do something nice for you or the kids," Emily said.

"Don't hold your breath," Steve said. "Any time he's offered to do anything with the kids, there's been a price tag attached."

Alannah and Steve's daughters Kitty and Jess, and Jody's daughter Leah came running over.

"Grandma, Kitty found something strange under the roses!" Leah said.

"Roses always make me think of my husband, Henry," Elsie said.

"So you've told us," Emily answered her. To the girls, she said, "Show me this strange thing you've discovered."

The children led her to the rose garden, where Kitty got down on the ground to point at an object hidden under the prickly bushes.

Emily bent down as far as she could, then got down on her hands and knees, knowing it was going to be hard work to get up.

She saw what appeared to be a metal box, with wires coming out of it. A screen showed digital clock. Emily didn't know for certain it was a bomb, but with her whole family there, she did not want to take risks.

"Girls, I want you to walk as quickly as you can. Don't run, but walk very fast out to the front of the house." She called out to the other adults: "Can someone please get Mum's wheelchair, and everyone walk quickly out to the front of the house. Just leave everything, and go, please. Right now."

Her daughters and son-in-law looked over at her, surprised by the tone of her voice.

On her hands and knees, Emily used her walking stick to try to push herself up. Steve grabbed Elsie's wheelchair and began pushing it. Kym came over to Emily and helped her to her feet, and looked under the roses.

"Is that what it looks like?" Kym said, warily.

"I don't know and I don't want to take chances," Emily said. "Let's just get out to the street in front of the house, and call the police from there."

It was the first time Emily had ever regretted the size of her huge garden. She wanted Kym to leave her and go on ahead, but Kym determinedly stayed with her as she walked slowly up the path.

They were the last family members in front of the house. Kym told the others what they'd seen, while Emily called Detective Carstairs.

In minutes, they were surrounded by vehicles with flashing blue lights, including a black vehicle labelled "bomb squad", along with curious neighbours, dozens of people in uniforms, and the two detectives who had visited the house before.

# Chapter 13: Fake

Emily had suggested the family all go home. They'd stayed.

The adults were now sitting in the lounge room, while the children were at the kitchen table, drawing.

While the bomb squad had left, forensics were still in the back yard, and police were still around the neighbourhood.

Detective Carstairs told the family: "So the bomb was a fake, or at least incapable of detonating. Bomb squad told me it was either a model or the most amateurish attempt they'd ever seen. It was probably meant to scare you."

"Then it worked," Emily said. "I was scared. My whole family was in danger, or I thought they were."

"You normally have a family barbecue on Sunday?"

"Yes. Well in good weather. Otherwise we have a family lunch inside."

"So anyone watching the house would expect your children and grandchildren to be here today?"

"I suppose so. I honestly never thought about it."

Kym said, "We shouldn't have to change our behaviour for this horrible person."

The detective sighed. "No, you shouldn't have to, but I suggest you do until we catch him. I suggest you do not do anything predictable. Don't follow your normal routines, and don't talk to anyone about any personal or family things. Don't post any information on social media. Be wary of what you say, even to close friends."

"How long would that be?" Kym asked. "How long would Mum have to put her life on hold? How long would we all have to act like our family life was some deep secret?"

"I can't answer that. I wish I could."

Emily asked, "So what can you tell us?"

"I can tell how he accessed your yard. As you know, your cameras are faced towards the front of the property, because that's where you expect people to come from. Those cameras didn't show anything. You don't have any facing the fences between your and your neighbours' yards. We've checked all of your adjoining neighbours' security footage. Last night, someone climbed the fence of the yard backing on to yours, and moved toward the back of their yard, so towards yours. Later that night a person, who appears to be the same person, climbed out over a side neighbour's front fence. This person didn't try to access either of those houses, so didn't set off anyone's alarms. The person was wearing a hoodie pulled down over their face, making visual identification impossible, so even if we find a suspect, we will have trouble proving he or she was the person who planted the device. We know it wasn't Jake Henderson, because we're keeping an eye on him while he's on bail."

"What happens now?" Emily asked.

"We will continue to look for both your father and your half-brother. We will also speak with your ex-husband again to find out if he has a alibi for the time the person was accessing the yards. Forensics will continue their investigation in your yard, and in your neighbours' yards."

"Well, that will make me popular with the neighbours and with Jack. Oh, I should tell you Jack's talking about taking me to court for a property settlement from the marriage, even though I had nothing at the time. Someone's told him he could get half of my current assets, not assets from the time we were divorced. He refuses to accept that's wrong."

"He really does seem to want money from you. Do you believe he could be U.N. Known? Or is there a reason you believe he couldn't be?"

"I don't think so. I think it's more likely to be my father or this half-brother I've only just learned existed. I just think if it were Jack, he wouldn't be able to stop himself from telling someone, but I can't be sure, can I?"

"No, you can't. Neither can we, so we will have to speak with him again. Have you thought of anyone else who could possibly want to extort money from you?"

"No, but as Jessica Flowers said, sometimes rich people attract attention from people who are envious or jealous or whatever. If it's just some random person out there who decided they deserved everything I have, then what?"

"We haven't ruled that out."

"What can I do to be safer?"

"You could consider hiring a private security company to patrol the grounds, particularly during the night, but preferably on an unpredictable, random schedule."

"Thanks. I will do that."

Steve said, "Alannah, Jody, Kym and I have been talking. We don't like you being here, with the way the threats are escalating. We'd like you to come and stay with Alannah and me. Kym's got room for Elsie and Jenny."

Detective Carstairs said, "That could be a good idea."

Emily said: "And if he's watching? If he knows where I live, he probably also know where everyone else lives. Me going to Alannah and Steve's house could put them, as well as Kitty and Jess in danger. I can't do that. I'm staying here. I will ask Jenny if she would like to go to Kym's house with Mum, or if she'd like to stay in a hotel, or whatever else. I'll tell Josh and Carole they can take time off if they want, and I'll still pay them."

"Perhaps you, your mother and your nurse could all stay at a hotel?" Detective Carstairs said.

"And then I might endanger hotel staff and guests, I can't do that," Emily said.

"Fair enough. Then I do recommend you get private security, and I will make sure there's an increased police presence in the area."

# Chapter 14: Insecurity

In the end, it was the staff who made the decision. They were willing to work as normal, despite whatever risk there was. Jenny said she was going to work weekends as well until it was resolved, so Emily's daughters would not be at risk.

Family Sunday lunches were cancelled until U. N. Known was caught. Instead, Emily and her daughters would have a Sunday afternoon online get together.

A private security company, Home Secure, began patrols.

For the first time, Emily started to feel isolated, having her beloved house and its verdant grounds as most of her world.

At different times of day or night, people in the Home Secure uniforms, with a a yellow sword and shield on the upper right sleeve of their blue shirts, would appear at the gate, and Emily or a member of her staff would remotely open the gate for them to enter.

"No visitors, and people in uniforms patrolling the grounds. Is this what it's like to be in prison or in a war zone?" Emily said.

"I've never been in either, so I couldn't say," Jenny answered. "But it's definitely uncomfortable. I hope the police catch this guy soon."

At the back door, Carole was talking to a security guard.

The guard asked: "I just need the toilet, can't you let me in?"

Carole said, "There's full bathrooms in the pool house, you can use them. That's the instructions in your contract. There's a kitchenette there as well that you can use in your break."

"The pool house is all the way at the other end of the yard! Just let me in for a minute."

"No. You're not to enter the house unless you're specifically requested to do so. That's what's in your contract. That's what your boss wanted."

"Just let me in, you bitch!" He tried to force the door open, but Jenny joined Carole in pushing back. They managed to get the door closed and locked it. The man started pounding on the door yelling.

Emily rang the head of Home Secure, Reg Jackson, and told him what was happening.

"I don't have anyone there at the moment. Can you switch to FaceTime and show me what he looks like?" Reg asked.

Emily switched the call to FaceTime, switched from the selfie camera to the main one, and went to a window where she could see the man.

"That bloke doesn't work for me," Reg said. "I've never seen him before. I'm on my way and I'm calling the police. I'll send some people I've got nearby, they'll get there first."

While the man continued to pound on the door and yell, Emily switched from FaceTime to recording, because this would probably be evidence.

Eventually, the man saw he was being recorded, left the door and came to the window. He started hitting the window while yelling that she had to let him in. The window was a sliding one, with a security screen behind it. Emily double-checked the security screen was locked and continued recording.

Multiple things happened at once. The man's fist went through the glass window, breaking it into shards, and slashing his arm. An alert at the gate showed the arrival of two security people, and Carole remotely let them in. Jenny ran to get the first aid kit. The security people, following the sound of yelling, ran to the back of the house, and tackled the man.

Once the security people had hold of the offender, Jenny went out with the first aid kit, and bandaged his arm.

Next to arrive were uniform police, followed by Detective Carstairs, and then Reg Jackson.

Jenny advised Detective Carstairs the man would need stitches, and should go to hospital immediately.

He refused to speak to the police, refused to give them his name.

Emily came outside and asked him who he was.

"You know who I am," he answered, as police led him away.

Detective Carstairs advised the man would be taken to hospital for treatment, before going back to the police station.

She took statements, and had Emily email her the footage, along with the front gate footage of the man's arrival. Reg confirmed the man was definitely not one of his employees, and pointed out on the footage where the sword and shield logo on his uniform was on the wrong sleeve.

When the police had finally left, Reg told Emily he wanted to do a full assessment of her home security, because she needed more than occasional security patrols.

"Is this going to mean my home feels even more like a prison?" she asked.

"A lot is going to be unnoticeable," Reg answered. "For one, you need cameras on all entrances, not just the front gate and front door. It wouldn't hurt to have a few motion activated cameras and lights in the grounds as well.

"Well, that will get lots of footage of foraging possums," Emily said. "Lights might startle them as well."

"And we should have alarms that come back to base at HomeSecure as well, including panic alarms for you and your staff."

"You want us to walk around with alarm buttons in our pockets?"

"They can be installed on the walls or under benches. One under your office desk would be good. You also want cameras and alarms on the pool house. It would provide good shelter to someone hiding. How often do you actually use it?"

"Mum and I both have hydrotherapy every day. Family use it when they visit, and Jenny uses it sometimes."

"And you go there alone?"

"Well, Jenny takes Mum, but I can get myself in and out of the pool with the pool lift. It's my own pool in my own yard, so yes, I go on my own, every morning."

"You definitely need cameras and alarms on the entrances."

"This all seems overkill. What's the minimum you recommend? I mean, if this guy is the one who's been threatening me, and he's in police custody now, do I really need all that?"

Eventually, they settled on cameras covering all entrances to the house, the pool house and Jenny's flat, as well as a couple discretely placed panic alarms.

# Chapter 15: Brother

Detective Carstairs called.

The man arrested at the house was Emily's half-brother, Henry Clark Henderson. He was alleging Emily had stolen his half of an inheritance of family money left by their father.

"So he knows for sure my father is dead?" Emily asked.

"He believes so," the detective answered. "We still haven't found any record. Has your solicitor found anything?"

"Not that I know of. I'll call her after I speak to you. Why does he think my father had money? He was a primary school teacher, at least when my mother knew him. They don't make that much money. Although if my father met up with his mother after leaving mine, he probably knows more than me about that. Maybe my father went on to have some other, more profitable, career."

"He seems to believe that his father stayed with your mother."

"Well, then he's sadly ill-informed about that, about any money from my father, and about anything else."

"He says he doesn't want to speak to us any more, but will only speak to you."

"Do you want me to talk to him?"

"Are you willing to?"

"Can I talk to Jessica before I make a decision?"

"Go right ahead. Get back to me when you make up your mind."

Emily called Jessica, and gave her an update.

Jessica advised that a wider search of records still hadn't shown anything further about Henry senior. "It's as if he just dropped off the face of the earth. Maybe he did die, but if he did, there's no record. Maybe he left the country. There's just no way to tell."

"So do I talk to Henry junior or not?"

"Have you considered telling him how you made your money? Explaining that you don't know anything about your father?"

"Anyone who really wanted to research would have found there was a five hundred million dollar lottery draw and days later I was rich. But that's not the whole story of my wealth. I've more than doubled that with careful investments. All my daughters have used some of it as seed money for their businesses. The win was just a starting point, it's not a whole story. If I'd still been married to Jack, the story would have been very different. Some people can begin with a fortune and end with a larger one. Other people can begin with a fortune and end with nothing."

"Well, I would recommend you talk with him anyway, maybe if the police can monitor the conversation, you can at least get a confession from him for the threats and the fake bomb, and everything, so he can go behind bars where he can't hurt you. And since you mentioned Jack, let me tell you, he has found a solicitor."

"Who has convinced him he's being stupid?"

"Sadly, no. I supplied the information. The solicitor tells me he has advised Jack they can't win, and Jack has instructed him to go ahead with the suit anyway."

"I ought to be impressed. I've never known Jack to be this committed to anything. Normally, he would have given up as soon as it started costing money."

"Before the solicitor contacted me for information, he made the mistake of telling Jack that costs could be awarded. Since

Jack is completely convinced he will win, he's also convinced the court will make you pay."

"So the solicitor is going ahead with this? Couldn't he just tell Jack he's not doing it?"

"He's a very young, inexperienced solicitor, just out of law school. I think he's afraid to drop one of his first clients. I know you don't need this in the midst of everything else, but we're probably going to have to go to court. It's going to be an unnecessary waste of time, and effort, I'm afraid. I'm waiting for them to put their application to the court to find out when it will be. Family court is usually not allowed to be published, but since people know who you are, it might leak out."

Emily sighed, and said, "Well, I've got nothing to hide, but can we avoid having the girls involved? They don't need that. They've already been scared by a bomb threat, and had our regular get-together cancelled. Their lives have been disrupted enough. Is there any way we can avoid disrupting their lives further?"

"They're witnesses. Their evidence can prove you had absolutely nothing when he left, the way you all struggled for years. They can explain that he gave you nothing to support them, and what their lives were like as a result of you trying to support them working part time so you could be a parent, and what it was like when you first got sick and couldn't work. The court will need to hear that. I hope we can just get statements from everyone, have the judge look at it and get a decision without everyone being called, but you never know."

"Is there any way we can avoid court at all?"

"Not if Jack's determined to go."

"Can we just pay him off, so I can deal with everything else that's happening?"

"You want to give him half your money?"

63

"Oh I don't want to waste that much. I know Jack. He doesn't understand money, and he doesn't really understand how much money I have, just that I have money and he doesn't. Make it a million, no, make it five million, if that's what it takes. But to get the money he has to sign something official to say I don't owe him anything, and he's not going to try this again. Oh and please, please, for the love of everything holy, please have him agree to never contact me again. Put some penalty in it if he breeches that. I don't want to give him money and then have him calling a week later asking for money for some other stupid thing. Is there any way we can do that?"

"Do you really want to give him that much money?"

"No. I don't, but I really don't want my daughters to have to go to court and give evidence against their father either. I'd pay to protect them from the extra stress after everything that's happened."

"So to protect them, you would pay him, even though it's obvious he owes you?"

"Yes."

"We might have to have some face-to-face meeting to sign everything. Can you handle that?"

"If that means I never hear from him again, I'm fine with that."

"How often does he call you now?"

"Two or three times a week, sometimes more."

"Do you mind if I add in a clause that says he has to go three months without contacting you before he gets the money?"

"Oh that is a good idea. Yes, absolutely add that in."

"Do you want me to come with you to the police station to talk to your half-brother?"

"Would you?"

"Of course.  I'll call Detective Carstairs and make the arrangements."

# Chapter 16: Meeting

The police interview room was crowded. Besides Emily and Jessica, there were Detectives Carstairs and Morley, Henry Henderson  and a legal aid solicitor.

Detective Carstairs began: "OK Mr Henderson. You said you would speak if Ms Clark were here, and she's here. Now, tell me about the bomb."

Henry moved uncomfortably in his seat, then said, "I didn't say I'd speak to you. I said I'd speak to her. I want everyone else out."

The legal aid solicitor was about to speak.

"I said everyone," Henry reiterated. "Otherwise I'm not saying anything."

"You don't have to go through with it," Jessica told Emily. "You can just walk out."

"I'm willing, if it's Ok with Detective Carstairs."

"It's highly unusual," the detective said, "but we can watch on the closed circuit camera from the next room.  At the first sign of any danger, to you we will be back in here. And you Mr Henderson will be handcuffed to the table while we're gone, to protect Ms Clark."

Henry did not resist being handcuffed.

Everyone else walked out of the room, leaving Emily alone with her half-brother.

"They're still recording everything, and they're still watching, so what was the point of having everyone leave?" Emily asked.

"Because i wanted to talk to you uninterrupted."

"OK, so talk.  What is all this about? Do you actually know for certain our father is dead? And why do you think there was an inheritance?"

"Oh, you know as well as I do our father had family money."

"This is the first I've heard of it. My mother never mentioned it. My father left when I was about a month old, and he hasn't contacted me since. I don't remember him at all. How did you hear about it? Did he tell you?"

"Of course he didn't tell me. You're lying. Do you ever tell the truth? He abandoned my mother and me to stay with you and your mother, even though she was old and ugly and horrible."

"He didn't stay with us.  When I first heard about you, and your mother I wondered if he had run off with her. I know the police were after him. I had Jessica, my solicitor, try to find him, and the last record of him she could find was your birth certificate.  So I don't know if he's dead or alive, in Australia or overseas, or whatever. So unless you actually knew him, and knew when he died, maybe your mother made things up, or he told her stories that weren't true. After all, she was a child, he might have convinced her of all kinds of things."

"No. My mother knows the truth. He was supposed to come and get us and he didn't. He stayed with your mother instead.  And I know he died and you got the inheritance, because you got rich suddenly.  I waited years for you to give me my share, and you still haven't done it."

"I didn't get any inheritance, and until the threatening letters started coming, I didn't know you or your mother existed. I only know now because of the records search Jessica has done."

"Oh so your mother didn't tell you what she did?"

"What my mother did? What did she do?"

"She made my father stay with you. You ask her. She wouldn't let him leave."

"Well, asking her won't help because she has dementia. All she ever told me, my whole live, was he left. She never told me anything about your mother or you. I never met him that I remember."

"You're lying. Where did the money come from then?"

"A lot has come from careful investments. The money I used for the first investments came from a gambling win, sadly disappointing, but true. How long have you been watching me? If you knew I was suddenly rich?"

"Always. Ever since my mother pointed you out in the street and said that was my father's other child, the one he decided to stay with. She told me my father was rich, and we should have been living with him, but because of you and your pig of a mother we couldn't. You were the spoilt little kid he stayed with, and I was the one he ignored."

"And you never once thought to just make contact? Send me a friend request on social media? Make a phone call? Write a letter the normal way and sign it instead of sending deranged notes on rocks through the window? And why would you manipulate your own son to help? Why did you leave him anyway? You clearly knew what it was like to be abandoned by your father."

"I'm not talking about any of that. I want to talk about my money."

"What money?"

"My share of the inheritance. I don't believe you didn't get it."

"There was no inheritance, even if he's dead. He was a primary school teacher. Surely you know they don't make much money."

"No. No. He had family money. My mother told me all about it. He was rich."

"Not as far as I know. I don't know any of his family. And I still don't see how you can know he's dead, if you didn't actually know him. Who told you?"

"It's obvious. You didn't have money and then you did. You got all the inheritance."

"And this mythical inheritance you've convinced yourself of is enough to threaten my family."

"I'm not talking about that."

"You're not talking about manipulating your own son to threaten me, about dropping a fake bomb in my yard, any of that?"

"I'm not talking about that. I just wanted to talk to you, so you know I know about the inheritance and how you stole it, so you know I know you took everything from me when you took my father."

"OK, well I don't think this is getting me anywhere. You're not answering any of my questions, and you won't listen to my answers to your questions. Detective Carstairs, I'd like to go now!"

The door opened.

Everyone who had been in there earlier re-entered the room. The duty solicitor said, "Well, my client still has not admitted to any crime, and I don't believe you have enough evidence, so you need to release him."

"He was caught trying to force his way into Ms Clark's house. He's not going anywhere until he's appeared before a magistrate. You can apply for bail then."

Detective Carstairs instructed Morley to take Henry to the watch house cells, while she walked Emily and Jessica out.

"I wish you'd managed to get a clean confession from him," the detective said to Emily.

"My client came voluntarily to help you. You can't blame her for not doing your job," Jessica said.

"Fair enough," the Detective Carstairs answered, "but I have to warn you, he's got a mention in the Magistrate's Court tomorrow morning, and unless we come up with some more solid evidence between now and then, there's a good chance the Magistrate will let him out on bail. The Police Prosecutor doesn't have enough to ask for remand."

"So we step up security at home," Emily said. "Reg at Home Secure already has big plans and has started putting them in place. We'll be ready for anything else he tries."

# Chapter 17: Threat

Emily took afternoon tea into Elsie's sitting room, and sat beside her.

"Mum, I don't know how much of this you understand, but everything is nuts, and I need to tell you about it anyway. You know Dad, your Henry had a son with his student, Kerry. That son, Henry junior is making life hell for me at the moment. He's been sending death threats. He put a fake bomb in the yard and scared me, made me afraid the girls or the grandkids would be hurt. He thinks Dad died and left me some kind of inheritance, but I never got anything. I don't even know if my father is actually dead. Now Henry's practically certain to get bail, and I don't know what danger we're all in, or how long he's been watching our house, or what other sources of information he might have. Now if my father's alive, and can help explain to Henry that he's wrong, I need to know. Mum, after Henry got that girl Kerry pregnant, what did he do? Where did Henry go?"

"Henry went away dear," Elsie said.

Emily tried not to groan in frustration. Instead she said, as calmly as possible, "Henry went away. Do you know where he went?"

"Henry treated that girl terribly."

"Yes he did," Emily agreed.

"A child shouldn't have a child."

"No, she shouldn't. That was very wrong."

"I knew then. I knew I couldn't trust Henry. Emily was just a baby, but she was going to grow up. She wouldn't be safe. I knew Henry had to go. I couldn't have him stay and be a threat to my little girl. Henry had to go. So Henry went."

"You made him leave? You threw Henry out."

"Henry had to go. Henry went away. He wasn't going to hurt my Emily."

"Thank you for that. You did the absolute best for Emily, always. Do you know where he went?"

Elsie looked at the vase of roses on a cabinet on the other side of the room. "Roses always make me think of my husband, Henry."

Roses made her think of Henry. Elsie had said it many times. "Why?" Elsie asked, "Why do roses make you think of Henry?"

"Oh hello dear, what's your name?" Elsie said.

"I'm Emily."

"I have a daughter named Emily. She's a lovely little girl, and I'm going to keep her safe."

"You're keeping her safe from Henry."

"Oh she's safe from Henry. Henry's gone."

"Do you know where he went?"

"He's gone away dear. He won't hurt Emily."

Emily tried a new tack. "The police are looking for Henry."

"Oh, yes, I know. They asked me. I told them Henry had gone."

"Did you tell them where he'd gone."

"Oh no dear. Henry was just gone. They can't find him."

Maybe she didn't know. Maybe she'd never known. There was another question to ask.

"Did Henry have money? Family money? Someone in his family rich?"

"Who dear?"

"Your husband, Henry, was he rich?"

"No dear. He was a teacher. He's gone now. Have you seen my little Emily? She must be here somewhere."

"I'll go find her."

Emily left the room. As much as she cared about her mother, dealing with her was difficult and sapped what little energy she had.

. . .

She was returning to her office when Jessica called. Jack had agreed to meet, and Jessica had drawn up the paperwork for the proposed agreement.

"I still don't like giving him any money," Jessica said.

"Neither do I, but if it buys me freedom from him, and saves my girls from having to go to court, it's worth it,"

"Well, we don't give him anything if he refuses to abide by the agreement, right?"

"Absolutely."

# Chapter 18: Agreement

Jessica picked Emily up. As they drove to the meeting Jessica explained that Henry had been granted bail on the charges of acting with menaces and trespassing. Police were holding other potential charges until they had more evidence. They were still unable to prove Henry had been responsible for the fake bomb, and the death threats. They did have enough to apply for a restraining order preventing Henry approaching her, her family, her home or their homes, work or schools, and order the magistrate had been happy to provide.

"So the upshot is, Henry's free, but if he comes anywhere near you or yours, he's going to jail."

"Honestly," Emily replied, "If he just leaves us all alone, I'm happy for him to continue to be free."

"The same as you're happy to pay Jack if you can be free of him?"

"Exactly. All I want is for my family and me to be able to enjoy a peaceful life."

"Well, I guess that's not a lot to ask, I hope it works out."

.  .  .

Emily and Jessica sat across the table from Jack and his uncomfortable-looking solicitor, named Bill Edwards.

"Although I have advised my client there is no way he could win in court, he is insisting on going ahead with this case. I'm not sure why we're here," was Bill Edwards' opening.

"I'm just surprised we're here without Geoff from Jack's work, who seems to be his actual legal advisor," Emily said, cynically.

"I was going to ask him to come, but he's been away from work for a couple of days. He's sick. But he should have come, he knows more about this stuff than anyone. I told him everything, all about you and all about the girls, and Geoff, told me I deserved the money."

Emily had a strange thought. Geoff, who Jack told everything to, was away just at the same time as Henry, who seemed to know more than he should, was in custody. "What does Geoff look like?" Emily asked.

"Why?" Jack asked in response.

"Humour me. Do you go out for drinks or anything? Do you have photos of you together? I'd like to know what this Geoff, who seems such an expert on my life, looks like."

Jessica gave Emily a strange look.

"As a matter of fact, we do go out sometimes. Geoff's a good bloke," Jack said. He pulled out his phone and scrolled through photos, and showed Emily a photo of himself with another man.

"Look familiar?" Emily asked Jessica.

"Henry Clark Henderson. So how does your half brother get a job under the name Geoff?" Jessica said.

"I don't know, but I guess we now know how he knows so much about my family. This is something we definitely need to tell Detective Carstairs."

"What are you two talking about? Emily doesn't have a half-brother, and Geoff's not someone named Henry" Jack said.

Emily shook her head, then said, "I don't have the energy for this. Let's just make the offer so we can leave."

Jessica took copies of the offer out of her briefcase. "It's like this," Jessica said. "If you go to court, Jack will lose, and will probably be ordered to pay Emily for all that he took from the marriage. Well Emily doesn't want that. She doesn't want to go to court. She doesn't want her daughters inconvenienced by having to appear.  So she's willing to make this one-time offer. Either accept it now, or it's off the table for ever. The offer is this: Emily will pay Jack five million dollars, on two conditions. Firstly, he will sign, here and now, an agreement that he acknowledges that this is a grace payment and that Emily does not owe him anything, and he will not under any circumstances attempt to claim anything further from her. Secondly, he will never again attempt to contact Emily by any means whatsoever. To be sure he will comply with the second condition, the five million will not be paid until Jack has gone three months without attempting to contact Emily. At three months, Emily will deposit the money into the same bank account she's been using to loan Jack money he hasn't repaid over many years. Decide now, because we're leaving in fifteen minutes, whether this is signed or not."

Emily was impressed. She'd never seen Jessica in full-on legal warrior mode. She prided herself on choosing good people, at least choosing good people since her divorce, and she was pleased with her choice in solicitor.

Bill seemed confused, but advised Jack it was the best offer he could possibly get, and he shouldn't throw away the chance to get so much money.

Jack said, "I think I should call Geoff and see what he thinks. Geoff knows about this stuff."

Jessica answered, "Well he was granted bail when he appeared in court this morning, so depending how quickly he was processed out of police custody, he might have his phone again now. Go ahead and call."

"What are you talking about?" Jack said.

"Geoff is a false name, of a man who has been threatening Emily, and your daughters and their children, presumably using information you gave him. But go ahead, ask his advice."

Jack hesitated a moment, looked from Jessica and Emily to his own solicitor, and back to his phone. Eventually he said, "I don't believe you, I trust Geoff." He tried to call, but received no answer.

"Guess he doesn't have his phone back yet," Jessica said. "Tick tick. Clock's ticking, make up your mind."

She began to pack things back in her briefcase.

"All right I'll sign," Jack said.

"You're sure you understand the agreement?" Jessica asked. "Do you need your solicitor to go through it and explain it paragraph by paragraph?"

"I said I'll sign," Jack said. "Where do I sign?"

Jessica showed him where to sign, Bill witnessed his signature, then Emily signed and Jessica witnessed her signature.

. . .

In the car, Emily said, "So did Henry seek Jack out? Is that the reason for the fake name? Or was it coincidence?"

"Him setting Jack up to try getting money out of you certainly wasn't coincidence. I don't know the reason for the fake name, or how he managed to get a job without being able to give a tax file number, which he'd need to use his real identity to get. Those are questions for the police."

Emily's phone rang.

"I don't believe this." Emily said, "It's Jack."

"What? I don't believe this either. Answer the call. Put it on speaker and record it."

Emily did as Jessica instructed.

77

"Jack, what the hell!" Emily said.

"That five million. Why can't you just give it to me now? This whole three months thing is nonsense."

Jessica answered, "Jack you just signed a document saying you wouldn't contact Emily again, and if you contacted her within three months you would get nothing. This is within the three months. It's so far within the three months it's utterly ludicrous. This call means you get nothing. I'm about to formally advise your solicitor that you now get nothing, and I will forward him a recording of this call. If you contact, bother, or harass my client ever again, I will get a restraining order against you, so that further harassment will get you sent to jail. I won't ask you if you understand, because clearly you don't even understand that question. Emily's hanging up now. Do not call again."

Emily hung up the phone.

"Email me the recording, so we've got a paper trail. I'll forward it to Bill Edwards, in case Jack wants to know why he's not getting any money. Then block Jack's number. If he tries to contact you in any other way, don't answer, just note it, block him, and let me know."

# Chapter 19: Letter

It was strangely quiet, blocking Jack's calls. Emily didn't know why she hadn't done it years earlier, except of course, she had spent most of her life with the kinds of phone it wasn't possible to block someone on, and had simply never thought of it.

One problem man dealt with, just one to go, she thought to herself, as she wandered through the garden, taking her time walking back from her morning exercise in the pool house.

She said "Good morning", to a security man who was walking the grounds. They chatted for a moment. His name was Tony. He talked about how much he liked this garden, and about his garden at home. He said he wasn't a great gardener, but he and his wife and children all had fun working on it together, as a family project.

Then Emily stopped to chat with Josh, admiring the roses, which were his pride and joy.

She chose some roses for her mother's room, and Josh obligingly cut them for her, carefully trimming the thorns. It was a morning ritual, choosing fresh roses for Elsie's room.

Today, Emily took extra pleasure in the little things. It was a gentle, relaxed morning. There'd been no contact from Henry since he had been released on bail, and none from Jack since she had blocked his calls. She hadn't realised just how tense she had been for months now. Except for the extra security, and her family not visiting, it almost felt like everything was back to normal. Almost.

She put the roses in a vase and took them to her mother's room, where Jenny was helping Elsie into fresh clothes for the day. Then she went to the kitchen to get herself a cup of coffee, took that into her office to check emails. She saw two letters in her in tray.  Since snail mail wasn't common, she decided to check those first.

The first was an invitation to an event an old friend was having.

The second was a now-familiar semi-legible scrawl. It said: "The next bomb won't be fake.I want my share.  I know where your daughters live and where your grandkids go to school."

Emily dropped the letter.  Her pulse raced, her heart pounding.  She struggled to breathe.  "Just a panic attack," she told herself, as she called Detective Carstairs' phone number. After that call, she called Jessica, and then each of her daughters.

It seemed only minutes went by before Detectives Carstairs and Morley were there, along with Reg Jackson.

Shortly after, Jennifer arrived.

The detectives took the letter, for forensics.

Reg Jackson suggested, if the threat were now against her family, perhaps the rest of the family should now come to Emily's house, since it was patrolled by security staff, and had all of the extra security he had installed.

Emily agreed to talk with her daughters, but asked if it would be an option to have security staff at their houses as well.

Reg said it was possible, but it would be spreading resources thin. He recommended locking Emily's home down with everyone securely inside.

* * *

Emily's family came to stay at the house. The children's school had been advised of the threat, and it was decided they should stay home for the time being. Reg doubled the security patrols.

While Emily was glad to see everyone, she was worried that having them all together might be what Henry had wanted, making them a bigger, more vulnerable, target.

Detective Carstairs rang to advise that on this occasion, Henry had made a huge mistake. He'd left a single fingerprint on the envelope the note had come in.

Police had gone to Henry's work to look for him, but he was not there. They found the answer to the question of his being called "Geoff" at work. He'd told the employer it was a nickname he'd gone by for years. The supervisor thought it was a bit odd, because man nicknames were a variation of a person's actual name, but didn't question it. So, while Henry's wages, and withheld tax were under his real name, he'd been introduced to all the other employees as "Geoff". The employer had noticed him cultivating a close friendship with Jack, but had not thought anything of it.

Jack was taken in for questioning once more, in case he knew his friend's whereabouts.

Emily thought for a moment about the call that would inevitably come from Jack, then realised she would not get that call, because she'd blocked his number. Even with with everyone in the locked-down house, she allowed herself a moment of relief and happiness.

Kym had brought art supplies, of course, and organised the children to paint a mural, on paper from a roll spread across the lounge room and along the hall. "Thought it was best to keep them inside," she said, as Emily inspected the work.

Alannah and Steve were in the kitchen, helping Carole cook dinner for everyone, and Jody was helping Jenny make up beds in the guest rooms.

With everyone busy, Emily was about to go check on Elsie when she heard her phone ring. It was an unknown number. Perhaps it was Henry, and she would be able to get information from him that Detective Carstairs could use.

She answered. It was Jack. She hung up. He clearly hadn't been questioned for very long. She sent a quick text to Jessica to tell her.

Kym's phone rang. Emily could hear her side of the call: "Yes Dad. ... I know your friend Geoff was actually Mum's half-brother Henry. We all know he was using you to get information about us. ... Yes, I heard you called Mum when you'd agreed not to, and now you're not getting any money. ... Well, if you'd listened to your lawyer instead of Geoff. ... No. I'm not home. Alannah and Jody aren't at their places either. ... The girls got pulled out of school. Henry, Geoff, whatever he calls himself threatened to bomb our homes and the kids' school. ... No, I'm not telling you where we all are. ... Well, how did he know where we lived? ... If it sounds like I'm blaming you, it's probably because I am. Good-bye Dad."

Emily went and hugged Kym, as she heard Alannah's phone in the kitchen ring. Alannah simply rejected the call. From upstairs, they heard Jody's phone ring, and Jody answer with, "Bugger off Dad, you almost got us all killed."

\* \* \*

They were packing away dinner dishes when Tony, the security guard, knocked on the door. When Emily answered, he said: "Your ex-husband's here. He says he wants to talk to you. Do I let him in the yard, or tell him to go away?"

Emily replied, "No-one here wants to speak to him."

Emily watched through the curtain, as Tony spoke to Jack. Jack turned to leave, but stopped to put something in the letter box.

Tony saw it as well. When Jack had left, he opened the letter box and picked up the parcel.

In an instant there was a loud booming noise, and the security guard seemed to spread out in all directions. The window Emily was looking through burst inwards, and shards of flying glass pierced her body.

# Chapter 20: Revelation

Emily woke up in her own bed, feeling groggy.

Jenny was sitting in the armchair beside the bed. "I persuaded Doctor Thompson to come here and treat you," she said. "Both she and I know how much you hate hospitals. The shock from the blast knocked you out, but then the doc gave you a sedative, to keep you relaxed while we patched you up. You've got a couple of deep cuts that needed stitches, but mostly it's just minor cuts we had to make sure there was no glass in them and dressed them. You've got a slight concussion, and I have to watch you for signs of your brain going squiffy."

"Brain going squiffy? That's the medical term? That poor security guy," Emily said. "His name was Tony. He had kids. Sounded like a nice family."

"Yeah, he wasn't so lucky. There wasn't anything anyone could do for him."

"I said hello to him this morning, it was just a normal thing. Then he died, working to protect me."

"And he did. If you had been closer to the bomb when it went off, you would have died too."

"And the family? Is everyone OK?"

"I told them you needed to rest and banned them from the room."

The door opened slightly and a small head appeared around it. "I heard talking. Is Grandma awake? Can we see her now?"

"Yes," Emily answered.

Jenny gave a disapproving look, but knew she would not win this argument.

Three small girls excitedly ran into the room and jumped into the bed beside Emily.

"Your grandmother's been hurt, don't be rough with her," Jenny scolded.

The girls were shortly followed by the Emily's daughters and son-in-law, who had heard the girls' excited chatter.

"This is too crowded!" Jenny insisted.

"You're right. I should go down to the lounge room where we will all fit more comfortably," Emily said. She kissed each small child and told everyone she would dress and join them downstairs.

Jenny helped her change into fresh clothes, carefully avoiding pulling or putting pressure on any of the many dressings.

"I'm getting the wheelchair, and taking you down in the lift," Jenny insisted.

"What happened to Jack?" Emily asked. "He wasn't far away when it went off."

"Far enough to not be here when the police arrived," Jenny answered.

Much as Emily hated it, she allowed Jenny to put her in a wheelchair, to take her in the lift downstairs to the lounge room. The whole family was there, including her mother.

Emily tried to make light of the situation. "I guess I need to get the glazier back in."

"I've already called," Steve said. "I hope you don't mind."

"Mind? Of course not." She reflected, not for the first time, that she was grateful Alannah had married a man as unlike Jack as it was possible to be. She looked around the room, relieved to see that everyone looked fine, if worried.

Jenny helped her move to one of the armchairs with the electric lift. Elsie was already in the other. As soon as Emily was settled the three grandchildren joined her in the chair.

"No crowding your grandmother. She's sore!" Jenny commanded. Her tone of voice would allow no argument.

The girls stood beside the chair instead. Emily suggested they go and grab some pillows and use them to sit on the floor, next to her chair.

Once they'd left the room looking for suitable pillows, Emily asked: "What have the police said? Surely Jack didn't leave a bomb by himself. Have the police caught Henry?"

"Oh no," Elsie answered. "The police won't catch Henry. Henry's gone."

"Grandma, we're talking about the other Henry," Jody said gently.

"Henry won't come back, ever," Elsie said, firmly. "I had to do it. He was a threat to little girls. He won't hurt my Emily."

"You had to do what?" Emily asked, afraid of the answer.

"Oh hello dear, who are you?" Elsie asked.

No. Of course there wouldn't be an answer. Before dementia set in, Elsie would never tell her anything about her father. Since dementia began, Emily had learned so much that she hadn't wanted to know, but could she believe her mother had killed her father? Was that what Elsie had just implied? Was it too much to accept? Perhaps she'd just forced Henry senior to leave. That's what it had sounded like before. What did "had to do it" mean?

Kym interrupted her thoughts. "Detective Carstairs said to call her when you were awake. She needs to come and talk to you. Shall I call now? Or do you want a break first?"

"Call her, I guess. I'll have time for coffee before she gets here."

Kym went to make the call.

Alannah said, "Mum, we've been talking, and would like to continue staying here until Henry, and Dad, I guess, are securely locked away. You still have better security than any of us. And none of us wants to spend their time wondering if everyone else is safe."

"I'm always happy to have you all here," Emily said. "I just wish the circumstances were better."

"Do you think Dad knew he was delivering a bomb?" Jody asked. "I mean, I refused to answer his phone call, and Alannah told him to bugger off, and Kym..."

"This is not your fault. None of it is. Who knows what Henry told Jack about that parcel. We all know Jack is easily manipulated by men he thinks are smarter than him. And Henry, he's completely off his rocker. No amount of facts or reasoning would get through to him. He's just not in touch with the real world."

\* \* \*

Steve took the children to the home cinema to watch a movie. Jenny took Elsie back to her room, for her afternoon nap.

That left Emily with her three daughters when Detective Carstairs arrived.

"I do need to interview you alone," the detective said, "but while you're all here I can tell you we have Jack in custody. He claimed not to have known the parcel was a bomb, but he wasn't at all clear on what he thought was in it. Once he was told we had him for murder, and that all of his children and grandchildren were in the house he blew up, he gave us a location for Henry. Unfortunately, Henry wasn't there."

"So Jack thinks he killed us?"

"He'll find out soon enough that you all survived. But for now, we're going to let him stew."

"I hope you find Henry soon. In the meantime, we have something else to tell you about. Something my mother said, makes it appear that..." Emily found she couldn't say the words.

"Grandma implied that she'd killed her husband," Alannah said. "But she might have just meant she made him go away. I mean we're not certain."

"Do you have any details? Where the body might be?" Detective Carstairs asked.

Kym answered, "Not really. It was really vague. Maybe we just all jumped to a conclusion, because she didn't actually say she killed him. She said she did something. She might have meant she somehow forced him to leave."

The detective said, "Well, if it was that vague, I think we should set it aside for now. We've got a much more immediate threat to deal with, and questioning Mrs Clarke isn't really going to get us anywhere anyway. So, let's just do your statement for now."

Emily led Detective Carstairs to her office, where she carefully described everything she had seen through the window.

She was exhausted by the time the detective left, but there was one more thing she needed to do before she could rest. She called Reg Jackson, and told him she wanted to pay for Tony's funeral, and to give some money to his family, so they would have one less thing to worry about.

# Chapter 21: Frying Pan

Alannah and Steve were cooking breakfast for the whole family.

Alannah called out to Emily, "Mum do you have any more frying pans? We want to cook everything in one batch, if we can, so no-one has to wait, or eat their food cold."

Emily answered, "There should be three stainless steel frypans, as well as the electric one, and if you can dig for it right in the bottom corner cupboard, there should be Mum's old cast iron one."

There was some crashing from the kitchen, as Alannah pulled out numerous pans to find the one furthest back in the corner.

Alannah came out to the dining room, where Emily and Elsie were having their morning coffee. She was swinging the cast iron pan, slowly.

"Hey Grandma, you really used this? It weighs a ton," Alannah said.

"Oh, I have a pan like that. I wonder where it is," Elsie said.

"You used to cook a lot of amazing meals in that old pan," Emily said.

Alannah continued to move the pan around, feeling the weight. "This would make an incredible weapon," she said. "If you hit someone on the head with this, they wouldn't get up again."

"No, he didn't get up," Elsie said.

Alannah looked at the pan disdainfully, and put it gently on the dining table.

"What?" Emily asked. "Who didn't get up?"

"Henry, dear. I didn't mean to hit him. I don't think I did. But I was afraid he might hurt my little Emily. She was such a tiny baby. I was afraid, and he was yelling, and I was cooking in the pan, and I just hit him."

"You hit him with the hot pan?" Alannah asked.

"He fell down. He didn't get up."

Emily asked the obvious question, "What happened then?"

"The only thing I could do, dear. I couldn't go to jail. My Emily needed me. I buried him."

"You buried Henry?" Emily was stunned. Although she'd suspected this after her mother's previous revelations, she was still stunned to hear it said so plainly. "Where?"

"Where what, dear?"

"Where is Dad's body?"

"Body? I don't know anything about a body, dear."

Of course she didn't. Emily sighed. She excused herself, went to her office and called Detective Carstairs.

The detective was there shortly after they finished breakfast.

Jenny wheeled Elsie back to her sitting room, to watch some television for a while.

Detective Carstairs said, "Before we get on to the reason you called me, I have to tell you the prosecutor dropped the charges against young Jake. There's enough evidence he was manipulated and didn't know what he was dealing with."

"I'm glad of that. He didn't need to be punished for what adults were doing," Emily said.

She went on to tell the detective about the conversation that morning.

The Detective thought for a few moments, then said, "Well, that's a clearer confession than the implied one earlier. She actually said she hit him with the frying pan and buried him?"

"Yes. Then when I asked where she buried the body, she didn't know anything about a body."

"It's not a lot to go on, and questioning her won't help. Do you have any idea where she might have buried him? Think hard, any place that was significant for your mother as you grew up. Either somewhere she spent a lot of time, or somewhere she avoided."

"Roses," Emily said quietly, and found she was crying.

"Grandma says all the time that roses always make her think of Henry," Jody said.

"She had a rose garden, in the house I grew up in." Emily said, " She wouldn't leave the place, not until it became obvious, even to her, that she couldn't live on her own any more. She looked after that rose garden so carefully. I always thought it was because she loved roses."

"Okay, I'll look into that. Try not to worry too much now. There may not be any evidence to back it up. We don't know if this was something that actually happened, or something your mother thought about. People with dementia can get very confused about things."

# Chapter 22: Discovery

It was strange to be back in her old childhood home, but Emily was determined to be here to find out the truth first hand. Jessica accompanied her.

Detective Carstairs had made them stay on the verandah of the house. With them was the current homeowner, a woman named Mary. Mary was very stressed, as police started to remove roses from the garden, to operate the ground penetrating radar machine.

"I'll pay for any restoration needed," Emily said to Mary. "My gardener, Josh, is a miracle worker. If the roses can be saved, he'll save them. Otherwise, I can buy you new ones."

"I don't think I even want to live here any more, if there is a body there," Mary answered. "If I've been living with a body in my back yard all this time, what does that say about me?"

"The same as it says about me all the years I lived here. It says you didn't know. If you don't feel you can live here, I'm happy to give you the current value of the house, so you can move somewhere else."

"So you'd buy the house your father was killed in?"

"No, I'd just give you the money. You could still have the house, sell it, rent it out, whatever. I wouldn't want to deal with it. I'll just make it easier for you to do whatever you need to do from here."

Mary sat quietly, seeming to think about the offer.

Emily focussed her attention back on the yard she had played in throughout her childhood, and at the rose garden her mother had so carefully tended for so many years. There were two people operating the machine, one pushing it over the ground, another looking at a monitor. The man at the monitor called out to the one pushing the machine to stop.

Then pointed out something on the monitor to Detective Carstairs. She nodded, then walked back to the house.

"I'm sorry," she said. "We've found something. It looks like human remains."

Emily tried to hold back the tears, as she asked: "What will happen to my mother?"

"No court is going to consider her fit to stand trial," Jessica said helpfully.

Detective Carstairs added, "I don't think she'll go to trial, but I'll have to check with my superiors, and probably with the crown prosecutor. We might have to charge her, if so, it would be up to the court. I'm with Ms Flowers on this one. I can't see any court forcing someone with advanced dementia to go to trial. We still have to go through with the investigation. Once it's over, you can decide if you're claiming your father's remains for a proper burial or cremation. Probably all this means is that one very old mystery is solved, and we can stop looking for Henry Clark senior."

"All these years, and he was only ever missed by a girl he'd brainwashed, and her son who she'd told lies to for his whole life. It's sad, really," Emily said.

"I need to get a tech to take a swab from you for DNA, just to be certain this was your father," Detective Carstairs said.

"In case my mother buried someone else under her roses?" Emily asked.

"Well, yes. We can't just assume things. After all the confession she gave you is doubtful, and we're not likely to get her to repeat it on the record."

Emily nodded, and agreed to the mouth swab. She was utterly exhausted. Somehow she'd hoped they'd find nothing there, that she hadn't the first twenty years of her life living next to the body of her "missing" father.

Before they left, Jessica gave a business card to Mary, and said to call when she'd decided what she wanted to do.

* * *

The fatigue hit on the car ride home. Every part of Emily's body felt as if it was dead weight. Her stomach started to have the uncertain feeling that she was going to disgorge its contents in both directions.

Jenny met them in the driveway with the wheelchair.

"How did you know I'd need it?" Emily asked, as she collapsed into it. She had no energy to say anything more as she was whisked to her bedroom, medicated and tucked in.

* * *

Emily was woken by a call from Reg Jackson, who wanted to upgrade her security further until Henry junior was found.

In a haze, Emily told him to go ahead and do whatever he thought was necessary, she didn't care what it cost. She found the mental energy to ask if Tony's family had accepted her offer. They had, and were grateful for it. Emily asked him to send her details of where to send the money, and she would give them a million dollars. It wouldn't replace a husband and father, but it would buy some financial breathing space to work out what to do next.

Hitting "end" on the call, she fell back into her pillow, and was immediately asleep.

Her sleep was troubled with dreams of roses, of bodies, of explosion, and shadowy men trying to terrorise her.

Some time in that long, weird, pain and fear filled, night, she decided to tell Josh to remove all the roses from her garden.

# Chapter 23: Court

Elsie had to appear before the Magistrate's Court for mention.

The Magistrate asked Elsie, "Do you know why you're here?"

Elsie replied, "Hello dear, what's your name?"

The Magistrate tried again. "Mrs Clark, do you understand this is a court of law? Do you understand this mention is preparatory to a committal on the charge of murder?"

"Oh dear. Murder, you say? Who was murdered, dear?"

"Your husband, Henry Clark."

"Oh Henry. He went away."

The Magistrate said, "Mrs Clark, I have a letter from your doctor. He says you have dementia."

"Oh hello, dear, what's your name?"

Jessica stood up. "Your Worship, I don't believe you're going to get any further with addressing my client. She was diagnosed with dementia some years ago. She now lives with her daughter, and has a live-in nurse caring for her. I would like to move that the court dismiss this matter, as Mrs Clark is now clearly unable to assist in her own defence."

The Prosecutor said, "The Prosecution is happy to accept that, Your Worship."

"Can either of you advise whether a psych evaluation would be of any use?"

"Both my client's doctor, and her live-in nurse have told me a psych evaluation would only confirm what is already apparent. Her nurse, her daughter and granddaughters are in the court today if you would like to ask them about her day to

95

day life. They assure me that while it is possible she committed the offence she is charged with, she is highly unlikely to commit any further offences. She rarely leaves her own room, and then usually only to see family members in the home where she lives. I'm also advised, there were extenuating circumstances at the time of the offence. Indeed there is a chance that were my client able to cooperate in her own defence, it would become clear she had an excuse at law. I am advised it was most likely she was acting in the defence of herself and her child at the time of the offence."

The prosecutor, said, "I agree that a psych evaluation would add little to what is already apparent. I'm sure if by some miracle the accused's dementia could be cured, we could present the charges again."

"Very well," the Magistrate said. "As the accused is in no state to stand trial, and unlikely to offend in future, the matter is dismissed."

That was it. Done. Elsie was free, as free as a person who almost never left their own house could be.

Jenny pushed Elsie's wheelchair, with Emily walking beside her. Behind them came Emily's daughters.

Outside the court, Detective Carstairs, who had been waiting in case she was called to give evidence, approached them.

"Jack is coming up for mention again later today. I understand he's being represented by the Duty Solicitor," she said.

"Don't look at me," Jessica said. I'm absolutely not representing him or arranging anyone else to defend him." She looked at Emily and said, "And I absolutely recommend you do not pay for his defence, Henry junior's either if he's caught."

"No, I won't," Emily said. "I might have if no-one had died. But that security guard's family have lost a husband and father because of them. It could easily have been a member of our family who died. They're both on their own."

Alannah said, "None of us are paying for either of them either."

"Good," Jessica said. "Taking care of Jacob was one thing. Those two are adults. They're responsible for their own actions."

"I have news on Henry as well," Detective Carstairs said. "He was picked up in Sydney trying to catch a flight to London. Given the charges, and the evidence, the interstate extradition will be a formality. So he will be here soon. You're all going to have to prepare to give evidence at committal hearings for both Jack and Henry, and then for their trials. I don't know if they're going to be prosecuted together or separately. So you could have a lot of court appearances to come."

Emily was exhausted as Jenny drove her and Elsie home. Alannah, Jody and Kym travelled separately.

"The girls will be able to go back to their own homes now," Emily said. "Even with all the danger it's been nice to have the whole family together."

"You can go back to having your family Sunday get-togethers," Jenny said.

"That will be nice."

"You're going to need to get a weekend nurse, you know. You and the girls can't keep looking after Elsie on my days off."

"I realise that. I might need your help to organise it."

"Once we get back, you need to go to bed, while I get Elsie down for a sleep."

"Absolutely."

That was when her phone rang.

She would not be going to bed when she got home. A worker from the Family Services Department would be by to bring Jake. He would stay with her on a trial basis, while the Department decided on his permanent placement.

"Are you really ready to raise another kid?" Jenny asked as Emily hit the button to end the call.

"The girls will help  Carole will help. You'll help, you know you will. We'll get by. He deserves a break."

"I guess he does.  And if I know anyone willing to give someone who needs it a break, it's you."

# Chapter 24: Family Barbecue

Emily and her daughters were setting the table in the back yard for the weekly family barbecue. It was their first since the bomb blast. They opened multiple dishes of salads and packets of buttered bread.

Jake pushed Elsie's wheelchair out to the back yard. "Do you want to look at the flowers?" he asked.

"Flowers, oh yes, dear."

Jake carefully pushed the chair slowly along the paths past the flower beds. He picked a geranium and handed it to her. She held it carefully, like a great treasure. Then he wheeled her up to the table, where Emily, Alannah, Jody, and Kym were. He left her with them and went over to where Steve was cooking steaks and sausages on the barbecue.

Emily heard parts of their conversation, while continuing her own conversation with her daughters.

"Need help?" Jake asked.

Steve put him in charge of cooking onions.

"What is it with barbecues? Do men always cook?" Jake asked.

"It's kind of an Australian tradition. Women cook inside and men cook outside. It's silly, really, because really everyone should learn to cook as they grow up. You should be able to feed yourself, whatever happens in life. I heard Carole's teaching you some basics."

"So why do you do the barbecue?"

"Because Alannah needs some time with her mother and sisters. I guess with her grandmother as well, as much as she's still with us."

Jake nodded. "So you're being nice to her."

99

"Yeah. If we were with my family, she'd do whatever she could to let me enjoy time with them. That's how families are meant to work. We notice what each other needs, and we look out for each other."

"I don't know much about those kind of families."

"I suppose not. You're with a good one now."

"All the years I wished I knew my father. Then when he found me, he didn't even tell me who he was. He tricked me into sending death threats to Emily. Now he's in jail. Everyone's saying he'll get life. Does that mean, like, he'll never get out?"

"More likely twenty to twenty-five years, if he behaves."

"Am I going to have to visit him?"

"Not if you don't want to. If you do want to, one of us will take you. It's your choice. We're all going to support you, whatever you want to do."

"And Alannah's father's going to jail too."

"Well, Jack was never much of a father. Alannah, Kym, and Jody, only ever heard from him when he wanted something from them. I don't think anyone's really going to miss him. I look at Jack as an example of what not to do as a Dad."

"And Elsie killed my grandfather."

"That one was a shock for everyone. I never would have guessed that. But she did it to protect Emily. That makes sense to me. Emily would do anything to protect her daughters. Alannah and I would do anything to protect Kitty and Jess, and Jody would do the same for Leah. That's what good parents do. They protect their kids, even if they put themselves at risk."

"My mother was in and out of jail as long as I can remember. I don't remember her doing anything for me. None of the foster families I've been with would do anything to protect me."

"But Emily got you a lawyer and stood up for you, even before she knew you were her nephew. When she found out who you were, she applied for custody. I know you've been through the wringer. You're safe now. You've got the rest of your life to learn what it's like to have a family who cares for you."

"Yeah." It was a hesitant "yeah," as if it was something Jake was still not entirely sure of.

Kitty came running. "Uncle Jake, push us on the swing please."

"Uncle?"

Steve said, "It was easier than 'Mum's cousin'. Go. I've got this."

Jake went to the swing set to push the girls.

Steve continued to cook the lunch.

Meanwhile, Emily and her daughters admired the flower Elsie was holding, and reminded her who they all were. They knew, of course, that she would promptly forget.

They also talked about Jack and Henry both being in jail awaiting trial. Emily's daughters insisting she hold strong on her decision to refuse help to either.

"They deserve everything that happens to them," Jody said. "It was different helping Jake. He's a kid, and he trusted the wrong person. Dad and Henry are adults, and they are responsible for their actions. They killed that man, and they could have killed any of us."

"Yes." Alannah added, "I know Dad claims he didn't know what Henry was doing, but you'd told him and Jessica told him, and we'd all told him, and he still delivered that bomb. He made his choices."

101

Emily started putting salad on Elsie's plate. "No. I really won't help either of them. I helped Jake because he is a kid, and because he had no adults in his life to help him work it out. And I helped Mum because I absolutely know she was protecting me. She did the wrong thing for the right reasons." She looked at her mother and sighed, "I can't imagine what it was like living with that secret for so long. It must have weighed so heavily on her."

In a short while, Steve brought the hot food to the table. Jake and the children joined them.

"Grandma, Uncle Jake can push the swing so high. It was like I was flying," Leah said, excitedly.

The adults were all duly impressed.

Everyone ate, talked and laughed.

Jake occasionally looked around the table in wonder at how this group of people could all just care for each other like this, and want to be together. He also wondered at himself. He felt safe. He felt at home.

Emily looked around at her family, grateful that all the trauma was over. Her gaze lighted on Jake and she gave him a smile. She was happy to see how quickly he was finding his place in the family, and happy to see that he had started to see Steve as a male role model.

The sun had started to go down, when they began to pack away the dishes and leftovers. As Emily cleared Elsie's plate, she noticed her mother had not eaten much. Elsie'd been eating less and less lately.

Kym went to push Elsie's wheelchair back to the house.

"Asleep Grandma? Overdone things, have you?" Kym said.

She patted Elsie on the shoulder, and her head flopped. Kym shook the shoulder a little, "Grandma!"

Elsie was unresponsive. Emily put down the plates she was stacking, and approached Kym and Elsie. She put two fingers on Elsie's neck to check the pulse. There was none.

Emily felt the tears coming, as she patted her deceased mother's hand. "You lived with those awful secrets for so long, to protect all of us. It must have cost you a lot. You deserve your peace now."

# Other Stories
## Scam Caller

The phone rang.

"Answer," Claire commanded.

The voice on the other end was unfamiliar.

"Hello I'm Mary from Hendricks Investment Mentoring. We provide mentoring on investing in the stock exchange."

"Oh," said Claire.

"I'm calling about setting you up with a mentor to get you started on your own path to wealth and security."

"Oh, OK."

"You will have me as your personal mentor, and with the help of our exclusive software, you can invest in the stock market and maximise profits. Some of my clients have doubled their money in only a couple of weeks."

"That sounds expensive."

"Not at all. For only a hundred and fifty dollars, you can get started trading shares on the Australian Stock Exchange. Your investment just increases and increases."

"Well, that does sound good, but I don't know where to find a hundred and fifty dollars."

"Of course you do. Half my clients are pensioners and they can find the money, surely you can too."

"But the judge said I'm not allowed money anymore. You'd have to talk to the person the judge said had to manage my money. The judge knows who that is, you could ask him."

"What?"

"My psychiatrist, would know too, but I can't ask him. Then he'd know I've got a phone and I'm not supposed to have one."

"Excuse me?"

"They don't want me to harass the victims' families."

"The what?"

"Would I need a computer for your software? I don't have a computer either. They confiscated it. I took pictures, you see. Pictures I kept on the computer. So much blood. Beautiful blood. I'm not allowed a computer anymore. I used my computer to find them. I could find you if I had a computer."

"Ahhh...."

"You sound like a nice person Mary. Where do you live? Are you near here?"

"I'm not allowed to tell clients where I live."

"Oh, but I'm not a client. I can't be. I don't have any money. And I don't have a computer for your software. But I do have a mobile phone and an escape plan. Can I come and visit you when I get out?"

The line went dead.

Howard walked from the kitchen with a cup of coffee.

"Scam caller?" he asked

"Scam caller." Claire answered.

"Psycho serial killer, multiple personalities, or little old lady who doesn't understand what they're talking about?"

"Psycho serial killer."

"You have way too much fun with scammers."

He put a straw in the coffee cup, and raised it for her to drink.

Unable to move any body part lower than her chin, Claire sipped the coffee, then made a point of moving her eyes to look all around her, and particularly down at her paralysed body.

"Since the fall, I'm not going rock climbing or doing anything else much at all," she said. "I've got to entertain myself somehow. And anyway, someone who claims to be able to mentor people on using the stock market and doesn't know you need a minimum of five hundred to make your first buy on the ASX is deserves to be trolled."

# Life Support

She woke slowly. The pain at the back of her head was black, overwhelming, drawing her in, like a black hole pulling everything into itself.

"Open your eyes", she commanded herself. She tried to obey her own demand. Slowly she opened her eyes. Stark, white light burned its way from her retinas through to the black hole at the back of her head.

She closed her eyes again.

Where was she. She could smell hospital - the strange smell of disinfectants and medication. It was a sterile plastic smell. There was a hum of some kind of machinery, a bip-bip-bip that could have been a heart monitor, a woosh, woosh that must be some sort of pump.

She wanted to rub her sore eyes, but her hands were stuck where they were, about 45 degrees from her body on either side. She tried to pull at them. Her wrists were somehow restrained, they would not move. The restraints weren't tight, but they were secure. She was effectively trapped.

Was there anyone else around? She wanted to call out, but there was something in her mouth, something she couldn't move. She was aware of something in her nose as well - and lots of something sticky holding this in place.

She slowly opened her eyes part-way, not to let in so much light, just a bit.

Definitely in a hospital room. There seemed to be tubes attached to her every orifice, and some that had been attached in places the orifices had to have been created.

How long had she been here? Had she had surgery? Had she lost the baby? Why couldn't she remember?

She so wanted to touch her belly, to feel where her son was growing.  Why must her hands be restrained?

"You're awake?" It seemed more a question than a statement. The quiet voice came from somewhere outside of her field of view.

In a moment, a young woman wearing pink surgical scrubs appeared and was looking down at her.

"Mrs Thompson? Mary? You're really awake?"

Mary tried to answer, but couldn't because her mouth was uncomfortably clogged.

"You've got a tube in your throat.  We'll have that out as soon as a doctor approves it."

Mary tried to move her hands, to show that she wanted her restraints removed.

"Your muscles have atrophied.  You haven't used them for a long time. It's OK, a physiotherapist will help you with that. You'll be able to move your arms and hands again, even walk again. It will take some work, but it will be OK."

How long could she have been here? What about her baby? She had been at 38 weeks, could she have been here so long he was due now?

"I'm just going to the other side of the room to phone the doctor," the nurse in the pink scrubs said.  "I won't be far away."

Mary struggled to hear the nurse's quiet voice becoming much quieter as she talked to someone else, somewhere out of sight.  She could not make out any words, just a sense of urgency. Was there something wrong? Had she lost the baby?

The nurse was back.  "Doctor says I can go ahead and take that tube out of your throat straight away. It's going to be a bit uncomfortable, I'm afraid.  Doctor Kayley will be here soon. Oh, I'm Lisa, by the way. Just relax, this is going to be unpleasant."

"Unpleasant" and "uncomfortable" did not begin to describe the trauma Mary experienced, as it felt like the tube was being pulled from right inside her chest to the outside world.

Tears were running down her face by the time Lisa said, "That's it. Over now. So sorry about that." Lisa gently dabbed up the tears with a tissue.

Mary tried to speak, but what came out was a croak, her throat felt like it was being rubbed with coarse sandpaper.

Mary tried again. "Husband," she managed to rasp. She suddenly felt exhausted from the effort.

"I'll call your family as soon as Dr Kayley's seen you," Lisa said, smiling gently.

Mary tried to smile back. She wasn't sure she'd succeeded. Even her facial muscles seemed incredibly unresponsive. Lisa would call Mark. Mark would make everything right. Mark was the kind of man who always made everything right. He was always so strong, so confident.

A tall, young, blonde woman in pink scrubs with a stethoscope hanging from her neck came into Mary's field of view.

"Hi Mary, I'm Sarah Kayley. I'm the Registrar here in Intensive Care. Let's take a look at you."

The doctor shone lights in her eyes, listened to her chest, poked and prodded, and hit her joints with a small hammer-type device.

"I don't know what to tell you, Mary. You're a medical miracle. I know you don't feel like it at the moment. You've been in a coma."

"Baby?" Mary croaked.

"The baby was fine. He came through the delivery perfectly. You were the one who had the problem. Your blood pressure went up out of control. You had a seizure, and you slipped into a coma. You've been here in the ICU since then. It's OK. You're going to be fine now. We're going to take care of you for a while, get you eating real food again, things like that, and then you can go to rehab."

Mary managed a very weak smile. She was exhausted, and found herself falling asleep.

When she opened her eyes again, the black hole at the back of her head was hurting a little less, and she found she could open her eyes a little more.

Two men were beside the bed. They looked familiar. One looked like Mark's father, and the other looked remarkably like Mark had done when they first met, in college.

The older man, gently put his hand over Mary's. "I never gave up hope," he said, tears forming on his face and in his voice. "Darling, I want you to meet David, our son."

# Cindy

A long time ago, in a place far, far away.

No. Sadly no. This wasn't long ago, at all, and not all that far away. It's the story of Cindy Castarella, no, not Cinderella, although their stories were strangely similar.

Cindy was exhausted. Caring for two children, doing housework, and trying to do grade twelve all at once was getting to her.

It hadn't always been like this. Cindy had been an only child, and had been very much loved by her mother, and at least tolerated by her father.

Then, when Cindy was fourteen, her mother had become seriously ill. Cindy had been her mother's primary carer through the cancer which had been diagnosed too late. Taking all her time with her mother for most of a year, had made it necessary to repeat a year of high school, but at the time, Cindy felt it was worth it to have those last months with her mother.

The day after her mother's funeral, her father moved his new girlfriend and her two children into the house.

Almost instantly, Cindy became unpaid maid and nanny.

Now, about to turn eighteen, Cindy had walk the two young children, who she sometimes suspected might actually be her half-siblings rather than step-siblings, to the primary school, before running to the high school. The children were not to be left until after the first bell, which meant Cindy was almost always late for her own school. She was tired of having to explain it to her teachers.

In the afternoon, she ran from her school to the primary school, where the two children would be waiting impatiently.

They couldn't go to after school care. Not her stepmother's precious babies.

After getting the children home, she would do washing and housework, while trying to help the kids with their homework, before cooking dinner for when her father and stepmother came home.

Then she would have to get the kids ready for bed. It was only after they were asleep that she was allowed to do her own homework.

Her stepmother had made it clear she hated Cindy, and constantly criticised the quality of her housework, her failings in caring for the children, and her just generally being a waste of breathable air.

When Cindy had asked permission to get a part-time job, her father and stepmother had told her she would need to pay someone to look after the children while she worked. As childcare would cost more than Cindy could possibly earn, this made the whole thing impossible. Cindy had made the mistake of saying this seemed very unfair, which sent her stepmother into a rage.

The stepmother was sick of Cindy's entitled attitude while she lived under their roof and ate the food they provided. She was so sick of it in fact, that she wanted Cindy to move out as soon as she turned eighteen and was no longer her father's responsibility.

Cindy was faced with a clock ticking down. In a matter of months she would have to move out, but in the meantime she was unable earn any money to arrange a place to go. She was still half-way through grade twelve, which didn't help her employment prospects or availability.

While reading a bed-time story to the children, she thought sadly that it was a pity fairy godmothers weren't real, and magical beings never came to her rescue.

Cindy didn't own a mobile phone. She didn't have money to pay for one. Her father and step-mother had them, but decided Cindy would only waste money if she had one. They kept the old landline phone, so her father and step-mother could contact her if needed to give her instructions for work they needed her to do.

One afternoon, the phone rang, startling her as she was walking past with a full washing basket.

The person on the phone said her name was Maureen, she had been her mother's solicitor.

"Since you're almost eighteen, I thought we should talk about what you want done with your trust, when you take it over for yourself," Maureen said.

"What trust?" Cindy was genuinely confused.

"Your mother's money. She left everything to you; her money the house, the car. That's what's been paying your school fees and your allowance."

"I go to a state school, there's no fees, and I don't get an allowance," Cindy said. "Maybe you have the wrong number?"

Now it was Maureen's turn to be confused. She named a school, and Cindy said that was the school her step-siblings went to.

Maureen said Cindy's father had been submitting receipts regularly claiming they were for Cindy's education. Cindy had not been receiving a thousand dollars a month allowance, nor had she been to camps and other things the step-siblings had actually done.

"What about your mother's jewellery?" Maureen was past confused and working her way to angry.

"My stepmother kept the bits she liked, and the rest I think my father sold."

113

"Let's make this simple," Maureen said. "You haven't received anything except meals and a place to live, which is your own house anyway?"

"No. And they've told me I have to move out as soon as I turn eighteen."

"I'm so incredibly sorry," Maureen said. "I just trusted your father, and reimbursed the expenses he sent. Tell me, would you want your father and step-family living with you if you had the choice?"

Cindy didn't even have to think about it. No. If she had the choice she'd live on her own and not have to be responsible for anyone else's cleaning or cooking or parenting.

"You're almost eighteen. My responsibility ends then, though clearly I haven't fulfilled it properly up until now. If you want, I can continue on as your advisor for a while until you find your feet taking care of your own investments. In the meantime, I have to fix as much as possible of what I've foolishly allowed to happen."

Maureen ascertained when Cindy's father and stepmother would arrive home, and told Cindy not to tell them she was coming. This would have to be a surprise.

That afternoon, Cindy finished the washing, and cooked dinner. She tried not to let on how excited she was. It didn't matter, no-one paid any attention to her anyway.

After dinner, her father and stepmother were watching tv, and Cindy was doing dishes while trying to get the children ready for bed.

There was a knock at the door.

Neither of the adults moved, so Cindy went to answer it.

There was a woman about her mother's age, and two very large uniformed police officers.

114

"Hi Cindy, I'm Maureen," the woman said. "I need a word with your father and stepmother, then we can talk."

Cindy led the visitors to the lounge room. Her father choked on his beer.

"Hi Clark," she said to him. "I don't think we've met, I'm Maureen, the solicitor managing Cindy's trust," she said to Cindy's stepmother.

"Ah, I'm Claire. I think you're mistaken. Cindy doesn't have a trust. She doesn't have anything."

Cindy's father buried his head in his hands.

"Claire would you be the owner of this bank account?" Maureen asked, showing Claire a bank statement.

"Yes. That's the account Clark puts spending money in for me."

"Hmm, well Clark told me he set that account up for Cindy, and I've been putting her allowance in it each month. According to my records you owe her forty-two thousand dollars. I'm sure you'll pay that back. How about we give you until her birthday to refund the money, before we press charges? Now these school fee receipts? Whose are those?"

Clark got up from his seat, a police officer moved closer and suggested he sit back down.

Cindy's stepmother looked from her husband to Maureen and back again. "My children," she said at last.

"Well, you see, I've been reimbursing these for three and a half years, on the basis of Clark saying these were Cindy's school fees. So that's another six and a half thousand one or other of you owe to Cindy, and again, as her trustee, I will give you until I have to hand the money over to Cindy on her eighteenth birthday to pay it back before we press charges. Now, the jewellery Ellen left to Cindy, I presume you can produce that, Clark? Keeping it safe for her until she's reached adulthood?"

Clark shook his head. He confessed to selling some of it, and to giving the rest to Claire.

"Well then, what's been given to Claire can be restored immediately, I hope. I have an inventory. I will leave it up to Cindy whether she wants to be reimbursed the value of what's been stolen, or if she wants to have you charged with the theft."

Cindy, suddenly realising she had a say, said, "I'll take the money. Claire still has the pieces that Mum wore most often, and pressing charges won't get the rest of it back."

"Very generous of you, Cindy," Maureen said. "And then there's just one other thing. I rang Cindy this afternoon and asked her about the house."

Claire gasped.

"I have here an eviction notice. Cindy, you just need to sign here," she handed several copies of the paper and a pen to Cindy and showed her where to sign.Then continued."This is your notice of eviction," she handed a copy to Clark. "By law you usually have to have thirty days' notice. I've filed an application with the court to make that immediate on the basis of your ongoing exploitation of Cindy. That was granted, but of course you can lodge an appeal when the court opens in the morning. In the meantime, these police officers are here to remove you and the children from the premises. I've been granted temporary guardianship of Cindy until she turns eighteen. Again you can appeal, but by the time that gets sorted out it will be her birthday. So you no longer have any responsibility for her and have no reason to be in her house or access her money. Oh, before I forget, do you still have her car?"

"Claire didn't like it, I sold it and bought her a new one," Clark said quietly.

"You want the money or to press charges on this one?" Maureen asked Cindy.

Cindy, who was starting to enjoy herself said, "I'll take the money again. Pressing charges won't get Mum's car back."

"And all of Ellen's clothes and other personal items? Cindy did inherit everything after all."

"All gone," Clark admitted quietly.

"I'll let them off that," Cindy said, smiling graciously.

"And Cindy has the phone her trust has been paying for?"

Clark shook his head. Claire pulled her phone out of her bag, and handed it over. "I suppose this is the one," she said quietly.

"How about you reimburse Cindy that as well, and we'll get her a new one?" Maureen said.

Claire nodded, and put the phone back in her bag.

"Well, then," Maureen said to Clark and Claire, "I suggest you pack up what you need for tonight, and tomorrow we can negotiate when to give you access to collect your other possessions. Let me know where you're staying, and I'll deliver an invoice for the money you owe Cindy."

Clark, Claire and the two children were ushered out of the house by the two burly police officers.

In the quiet after they left, Maureen listened to Cindy as she talked about the life she'd lived since her mother died. Then they began to discuss and plan for the future Cindy at last discovered she could have.

# Gone to Sea

Father has gone to sea again.

I asked why we couldn't go with him.

He put me on his lap and said, "Flora, you are a little girl. The sea is no place for girls or women. It is far too hard and dangerous. You must stay here, on land, where it's safe, and life is easy, with Mother and with Grace."

Grace and Mother and I went down to the dock to see his ship sail. We kept watching out until it was out of sight.

I asked Grace that night as we went to sleep, was the land really safer than the sea?

She said as far as Father knew it was.

Father was gone for a year last time he went to sea. He was only home for a fortnight before he left again. He said that was how long it took to offload cargo and re-provision the ship. He said that was long enough for all the younger men to spend all of their pay.

While he is gone I am learning my numbers and letters. Mother taught Grace and now Grace teaches me. Our island does not have many children, so it does not have a school. It is mostly a place where ships are provisioned on their way to somewhere else. Not many families live here.

Apart from my lessons, I have my work to do. I must fetch the water. It is a long walk, because I have to go to the part of the creek where there are no crocodiles, and the bucket is too heavy for me to carry it full, so I have to do a lot of trips. Mother says to make lots of noise on the walk, so the snakes know to stay away. I have to feed the chickens and collect the eggs. I have to feed the goats. Mother says when I am bigger I will have to help with the milking.

Grace milks the goats, and digs the garden to plant the vegetables. She weeds the garden and picks the fruit and vegetables. She also sews and mends our clothes, Mother is teaching her.

Mother sews clothes for other people, sells our fruit and vegetables at the market if we have grown more than we need, makes cheese and butter from our milk, and cuts wood for the stove. She says she is saving to buy a horse, or even a donkey, so she won't have to carry everything to the market.

Mother and Grace take turns to cook our food, and they are teaching me. I already know how to cook vegetables and eggs. Soon Mother is going to teach me to bake bread.

When Father is home we have meat, but only mother cooks that, because neither Grace nor I know how.

Grace says she will be old enough to marry in a couple of years, and then I will have to do her work, because she will have her own home to look after.

I told Grace that Father must get very tired if life at sea is so much harder than life here, because I am very tired here.

Grace said Father never stayed here long enough to know how hard our life is. Grace does not think very highly of Father.

I asked Grace how many crocodiles or snakes were on Father's ship, because he said it was so dangerous.

Grace said the real dangers on the ship were bad weather and drunken men.

I know about bad weather.

We had a big storm here once. It blew the roof off the house. We had to cut bark from trees, carefully, so as not to kill the trees, so Mother could use that to make a new roof. That storm killed half our chickens and one of the goats. In another storm, lightning hit a tree and cause most of our island to catch fire. Everyone who lives here was out fighting the fire and two families lost their houses. We all helped them build again, and shared whatever we could with them.

I know about problems with drunken men as well.

One day when I come back with the water, I found Grace screaming. A big man from the other side of the island was holding her down. He smelled like rum. I know the smell because Father drinks it.

Grace was fighting and screaming, and this man was on top of her, and I didn't know what to do, so I hit him with my bucket. There was water everywhere and the man had stopped moving, but his head was bleeding. Grace pulled herself out from under him, "You saved me," she said. Then she said, "Is he dead?"

I poked him. He didn't move. "He might be. I'm going to get into so much trouble. I killed a man. I will go to jail or be hanged."

That was when Mother got back from the market. She stood there and looked at us, and at the man on the floor.

"He was trying to force himself on me," Grace said. "Flora hit him with the bucket. She wasn't trying to kill him, just to stop him from hurting me. Please don't let Flora go to jail. I'll go in her place."

Mother said, "No-one's going to jail. Get the shovel."

We all took turns digging. We dug the biggest hole. Then we dragged that awful man and threw him in it. We filled in the hole. It took us all night.

Then Flora turned the dug up patch into another garden, and planted seeds in it. We don't eat the vegetables from that garden, and we never talk about why.

Sometimes I look out to sea, hoping to see Father's ship, and I think about the dangerous and difficult life he leads. I wish he could live on land with us where life is so much easier and safer.

# Save Us

"We can do it," Suzie said, "just the way Grandma said."

"She used clay. We haven't got clay," Sally answered, keeping her voice quiet, so no-one outside the room might hear.

"We've got plasticine. That's like clay," Suzie said.

"That can't work, can it? Doesn't it have to be clay?"

"Grandma used clay, but she had clay. We've got plasticine."

Sally relented, and they formed a clump of plasticine into the shape of a human, or similar to human.

"It's a plasticine doll. It's not going to work. It's too small anyway," Sally said.

"We have to try. Our parents are in there." She pointed to the adjacent wall. The twins' parents were in the next room.

"OK, but it's not doing anything," Sally said.

"Because we haven't finished. Grandma said they had to write what they wanted it to do and then put that inside it."

Suzie wrote on a small piece of paper: "Save our parents. Save us."

They pulled the middle of the plasticine doll apart, rolled up the piece of paper, and reformed the doll's middle around the paper.

Then they watched, holding their breath.

The doll wiggled. It moved. It jumped from the desk it had been made on to the floor. In an odd gait, probably caused by having one long thin leg and one short fat one, it ran to the door, squeezed itself flat, and wiggled under the door and out of their sight.

The girls both ran the dividing the dividing wall. They pressed their ears up to the wall, hoping to hear what was happening.

There was a sound of voices, their parents' and the person who was keeping them in the room. The voices were too low to hear what they were saying.

Then they heard the sound of something smashing. A chair scraped on the floor, and a a yell was audible.

It seemed only seconds later, the door to the room they were in flew open.

Dad was in the door way, with the wriggling plasticine doll in his hand.

"A golem? The two of you made a golem?"

The twins, huddled together, both nodded.

Dad went on, "You know this is exactly the kind of nonsense the principal wanted to talk to us about, don't you?"

The girls were quiet.

"Your little friend broke the principal's favourite coffee mug, and dumped coffee all over her. She said that was the last straw. You know what that means?'

Two small heads shook side to side.

"It means we have to find you yet another new school. Come on. Get your things. We're leaving."

They met their mother at the door of the principal's office.

As the family left the school, the girls both hung their heads as if they were ashamed, but anyone looking very closely would have seen they were smiling.

# She Survived

Alice leaned back against the wall, her hand still gripped around the handle of the knife. There was blood, more blood than she had ever seen before.

She slid down the wall into a squat position. Putting her head down to her knees to avoid seeing. She wanted to let go of the knife, but her hand wouldn't cooperate.

The police would come soon. She had managed to dial triple zero, before Mark had smashed his way through the door.

In her mind she went back two years. That night when she was attacked on the street, when Mark, a stranger then, had rushed to her aid. He was her knight in shining armour, who had saved her. But, he hadn't just saved her, had he? He hadn't stopped punching that man once she was safe, he had kept going, far more than was necessary. She wanted to tell herself, the self who had been so frightened and confused, that a man who so obviously loved violence, would also use it against her.

Her throat hurt, she knew there would be huge bruises around her neck. He would have killed her. She had felt herself fading as those huge hands had crushed and crushed. He'd had her up against the kitchen counter, using his superior strength and size, choking her, as the world had started to slip away into darkness. Neither of them had seen the knife until she felt it under her hand. She'd reacted, not acted, not really knowing what she was doing, but desperate to stay alive.

Alice thought back to that first time he'd hit her. She'd spent the afternoon with her sister, when he hadn't given permission. At the time, she'd thought, "Why do I need permission?" But then unconsciousness had overtaken thought. If only she could tell Alice of that day, "Run, don't look back, leave your home, leave everything and everyone you know, just run and hide and never ever come back."

The light in her kitchen had changed. It was suddenly blue, then back to white, then blue again. Somewhere inside her brain there was an acknowledgement that blue meant something, but what that something was was out of reach.

She recalled the day when he explained that if she ever tried to leave he would kill her. She belonged to him and only him, utterly and completely. There was no life for her without him. If she could only speak to the woman she was then, she would say, "We need a plan. Don't just trust a restraining order. Paper won't stop him. Don't trust he'll obey the rules."

Somewhere, a long way away, a male voice she didn't know said, "Drop the weapon. Drop it. Drop the weapon or I'll have to shoot."

Another voice, a woman answered, "She's in shock. She probably can't even hear what you're saying. Put your gun away.

"Alice. Alice, it's over. You're safe now. Let go of the knife."

Alice, that was her wasn't it? This voice was talking to her. The knife. Yes, the knife. She was still holding it. Her hand wouldn't let it go before. She tried again, put all all the effort she could muster into opening her hand. The knife dropped to the tiled floor.

"That's good," the woman's voice continued. "Now, can you stand up? Do you need help?"

Alice tried to stand. Blood flowed into muscles that had been held tight for too long. The pain was almost unbearable. Her knees buckled.

Strong hands caught her as she fell. She was aware of the blue uniform of the woman who helped to hold her up. Blue light. Blue uniform. Police. That's what blue meant.

"Alice, the ambos are here now. We're going to take you to hospital. I'll stay with you. Once you've been checked out, I have to interview you. We need to record what happened here."

The police officer gripped her under one arm, someone else was on the other side, they walked her through her house.

"You don't have to look. Just look straight ahead," the police officer said.

In the ambulance, she felt a clip on her finger.

She heard a voice say, "Her oh-two is low."

A plastic tube was placed across her face, with prongs stuck in her nose. There was an overwhelming smell of plastic. The smell made her feel sick.

"Look at her neck," the voice said again. "Her windpipe's probably damaged. It's a wonder she's breathing at all. Then there's all these other injuries. What the hell happened to this woman?"

"She survived," the police officer answered.

# Through it All

Yet again, the phone rang. Yet again, she answered. Yet again, all she heard was static. Yet again, she hung up, annoyed.

She went back to looking over the old photo albums. Memories. Times long gone. Times that could never come again.

Again the phone rang.

"Just what do you want?" Carla yelled as she answered again.

There was static. Then a feint voice. "Carla. Carla. Are you there?"

That voice. It wasn't possible. It had to be some kind of sick joke.

"Carla," the voice came again.

"No." She said. "It can't be. Whoever you are stop this now."

"Carla," the feint voice came again, "it's me. It's David."

"This isn't funny. David is dead. I went to his funeral today. Whoever you are leave me alone."

She hung up.

The phone rang again.

"Carla," the voice sounded even more feint, as if it were getting further away. "Carla, please don't hang up."

She hung up.

The phone rang. She ignored it. She set it on silent.

She went back to the album. Photos of her and David. Photos of the good times. The times before it all went wrong.

Why did it all go wrong? Was there any way she could have changed things?

The doorbell rang.

She opened the door. Eric, David's brother, was there.

"I know you're not going to believe this," he said, "but I have to tell you anyway. I had a phone call. The voice. It sounded exactly like David, only somehow far away. I know it sounds crazy, but it was him. He said to tell you he always loved you. He never stopped. Through everything, he loved you."

# The Golden Orb

Every generation of the family had a Zelda. She was always single, childless, stonking rich, and mad as a hatter. That's how the story went.

This Zelda couldn't care either way about the "single, childless" bit of the family story, but she suspected that might change if she ever met a man who she considered worth her time. As for extreme wealth, she was pretty sure she could handle that. Being crazy, that part wasn't in her plans.

She was thinking about the family mythology and her place in it because the reigning Crazy Aunt Zelda had recently died. She'd been considerate enough to do so in mid-semester break. Working on her PhD thesis, Zelda hadn't planned to take the time off, but no-one really expected her on campus and she was free to fly home for the funeral.

She'd heard conflicting stories about Aunt Zelda's death. It was a skydiving accident or a snowboarding accident. It wasn't until she reached home, that she heard the full story. It was a skydiving and snowboarding accident. Aunt Zelda jumped out of a plane, with a snowboard and no parachute, planning to land on a snowy mountain and ride the board to the bottom. The "Crazy Aunt Zelda" moniker fitted well.

Zelda took her place in the first row at the funeral along with her family: her sister Mary, her parents, her Uncle Hueby and his sons Andy and Howard. The crematorium chapel was full. That was hardly surprising. Aunt Zelda had lived life to the full, and made lots of friends. She'd also given lots of money to charity.

All of the right things were said, and the family members placed white roses, directly from Aunt Zelda's garden, on the coffin before the curtain closed.

During the afternoon tea that followed the service, Uncle Hueby took Zelda aside.

"It's about Zelda's will," he said. "I don't know how to tell you this, little Zee, but she left everyone else money, shares, Mary got her house, but not you. She only left you this. I think you can contest the will if you want." He handed her a small wooden box, which had the letter Z burned into the top.

"I don't know what's in it. I couldn't get it open," he said.

"It's OK Uncle Hueby," she said. "I asked Aunt Zelda to leave me out of the will. She paid for University for me. She offered. I didn't ask. She bought my flat, paid my fees, and put aside money for an allowance for me so I didn't need to work, I could just focus on study. I told her if she did all that for me I didn't want to be in the will. This box must just be some small personal trinket she wanted me to have."

In her old bedroom at her mother's house, Zelda looked at the box that her uncle had been unable to open. She lifted the lid. It opened easily. Inside the box was lined with what seemed like black velvet and it held a small gold ball which seemed to glow. She reached in to pick it up, but her fingers went straight through it. A tingle went from her finger, up her arm and through her body.

Was it some kind of hologram? Zelda looked over the box. She couldn't find any power source. She picked up the lid. Tucked into the underside she found a card which had written on it, "My darling Zelda, with the orb in your possession, the world is yours." The card looked very old, perhaps a previous Zelda had written it to her aunt.

The flight home was more comfortable than expected. Zelda had been upgraded to first class because of a glitch in the ticketing system.

That night, she won the Lotto jackpot, a hundred and twenty million. She put most of the money into shares. Over time, she would discover that whatever companies she invested in would do well, no matter what was happening in the rest of the share market.

Everything she did simply worked for her. Her PhD thesis passed first time. She decided against a regular job, because she didn't need one. She tried art, and won awards. She tried writing, and won awards. She tried swimming and won medals. When she parked her car for too long, the parking meter malfunctioned and always showed she was in credit. It seemed it was impossible for her to fail at anything.

She began to realise why her aunt had seemed crazy to the family members. She could get away with crazy, seemingly-stupid high risk things, when she couldn't fail at anything she tried. The downside was she couldn't have a romantic relationship with someone when she didn't know if they would have freely chosen to be with her.

Zelda gave away huge amounts of money. She quickly discovered charities were like people; some could work absolute miracles with minimal resources, while others could spend an infinite amount and still achieve virtually nothing. She supported those whose work made the greatest impact. They seemed to be even more effective once she became a patron.

Then she researched her family history. As far back as she could trace her family tree, along the maternal line there really had always been a Zelda, just as the family story went. None of the Zeldas ever had a child, but each had a sister who had a daughter she named Zelda. And once the new Zelda reached her late 20s, the older one died in some kind of accident. It happened time and time again, generation after generation. Each of them really had been ridiculously rich, and had handed a great deal of wealth on to family members.

This Zelda documented everything she learned. Her niece, who she knew would eventually be born, would receive more than the box, more than the old card with the note. She would also receive all the information Zelda could find about the box, the orb, and the family history. The next generation's Zelda would start out better equipped to understand.

# The Seance

Mary looked across the table at Marcus. Her expression said it all. She was sceptical, more than sceptical, that this would work.

Marcus shrugged, and looked back at the medium. Her head was thrown back and her eyes glassy. For a moment, Mary wondered if they should stop holding hands and check Madam Zelda was still alive.

Then Zelda began to shake, and she called out: "Andrea James! Andrea James! Your children are here and they need to talk to you. Andrea James, speak to us."

In another voice, one that sounded eerily like their mother's, Zelda continued. "I don't belong here. You can't just call me back."

"It's kind of important, Mum," Marcus said.

"It's the bank," Mary continued. "They keep charging you fees. We've been in to see them. We've even given them a copy of your death certificate."

"They insist, they can only close the account if you sign the forms!" Marcus said. "Even though they've got your death certificate."

"And they say they'll sue us, as your heirs, if you don't pay the fees," Mary said.

"You called me back from Heaven to deal with the bank?" Zelda said in their mother's voice.

"We've got the forms with us." Marcus said, "Are we allowed to let go of hands so I can get it?"

"And how do you expect me to sign without a body?" their mother asked, quite reasonably.

"Well, if you can talk through Madam Zelda, maybe you can write through her as well?  That's what we were hoping, anyway," Mary answered.

"How much do I supposedly owe them?" their mother asked.

"Well," Marcus said, "you owed twenty-five cents when you died, but with interest and extra fees, they say it's five thousand dollars now."

"And they say if we don't pay, they'll sue us for that and their legal costs as well. That is unless you sign the form to close your account." Mary said.

"We did ask for consideration of special circumstances, you being dead and all," Marcus said, "but the bank manager said if being dead was a special circumstance, he'd have to cancel debts for half his customers."

"Well, we will have to try it then,  put the form in front of the medium."

Marcus slid the bank form and a pen across the table. There was silence for a minute or two.  Then, very slowly, Madam Zelda's hand lifted, she picked up the pen, and slowly, deliberately, signed the paper.

Madam Zelda sighed deeply, and spoke again in their mother's voice, "That's done.  I love you both, but now I really have to go back to where I belong."

"Thanks Mum," said Mary, " We love you too, and we have to go as well.  Zelda's got a long line of people waiting to sort out bank problems."

# Howl

When other women complained about their monthly cycles, Karen would nod sympathetically. She had a horror cycle of her own. Theirs contained blood, as did hers, in a way.

She was a captive of the moon. Its cycle was her cycle. For those five nights centred on the full moon, she lost herself, ran wild in the forest adjacent her back yard. Those nights in black and white were primal, wild, free, sometimes bloody. She hated them, she feared what she might do.

Those days she was exhausted, having not slept from moonrise to moonset. Those days all she could face eating was meat, bloody and raw. She ate all she could during the day, so she wouldn't be hungry at night.

She could not work during that week, so she was only able to work part-time, and supervisors knew she would be unavailable one week in four. "Medical complications related to her cycle" was enough of a reason for most supervisors. If any pushed for further she would tell them how truly terrible endometriosis was. She would never outright lie and say that she had it, only allow them to make their own conclusions. She did make it clear that she would be physically unable to stand at a cash register on those days, which was absolutely true.

This morning, Karen was standing at her kitchen sink with a saucepan of boiling water. Into the water she dropped her sharpest knife, a pair of tongs a needle, and some sewing thread.

She would need another pair of tongs to get them out. She boiled the kettle and poured water over the second pair of tongs and a plate. Then she pulled the implements from the pot.

This was going to hurt. She opened the wound on her abdomen a little further with the knife, trying not to scream from the pain. With the tongs from the saucepan, she reached in and pulled out the bullet. It hurt, but she was fairly sure that if it had reached any organs she would be dead. She stitched the wound closed. It would not leave a scar. At moonrise, all injuries would heal. Until then she would endure the pain along with the fatigue.

Nothing like this had ever happened before.

The bushland belonged to her family. The house and the forest had been in the family for generations, and family members all contributed to its upkeep because they all knew that any of them could produce a daughter or granddaughter with her condition. It sometimes skipped generations completely, but the lycanthrope gene passed through the maternal line. It was always women it affected, women were already tied to the twenty-eight day cycle. With puberty some of the girls of the family showed themselves to be normal women, and some to be lycanthropes.

If someone was on her property with a gun, they were trespassing. The property was currently ostensibly owned by her uncle, her mother's brother. He would never allow roo shooting or pig shooting on the property in the week of the full moon.

She couldn't call the police to report the incident. Too many questions would be asked. What if whoever shot her came back again tonight? She could heal from this injury but if she were shot in the head, or heart, there would be no coming back. Despite the legends, it didn't take a silver bullet to kill a lycanthrope, just an accurate one. Despite the legends, if she died as a wolf, she would stay as a wolf, and no-one, except family, would know what had happened to her.

Karen had only just got dressed again, when she heard her front door opening. She didn't need her heightened sense of smell to be overwhelmed by the cloud of perfume that entered. Grimacing in pain, Karen ran to the front room to greet the intruder.

A short woman in a bright yellow suit, with grey hair and purple highlights, looked surprised. "Oh," she said. "The owner said there wouldn't be anyone here. I'm Margaret Burns, from the real estate agency. I'm here to take photos for the ads."

"What ads?" Karen asked.

"The ads for the sale of the house."

"You must have the wrong address. This house isn't for sale. How did you get in? Did you pick the lock?"

"Oh, I'm so sorry. Didn't the landlord tell you he was selling? That's very unfair of him. I have a key, see." She showed Karen a key, that could very well have been a copy of her front door key.

"There is no landlord," Karen said. "I don't know how you got the key, but this is my home. It's been in my family for generations. Now leave before I call the police."

"Oh dear." The real estate agent answered, "I will get back to the landlord, and have him explain it to you."

The woman, appearing flustered, left.

Karen phoned her uncle. He assured her he had not hired any real estate agent and had no idea what was happening. He would, however, look into it.

Despite the assurances, Karen was restless. She ate a large rump steak before lying down and trying to rest before the moon called her again.

Eventually she drifted off, and knew nothing with her human consciousness until the next day.

She had no real memory of the night, just flashes. The trees, a man, a gunshot, blood, so much blood. The taste of warm raw meat.

A day later, her uncle was reported missing.

The next week, police searched her forest, because they'd run out of other places to search, and no one gave up searching for missing rich men.

Her uncle's body was found, with injuries resembling an animal attack, and with an unlicensed firearm in his possession. Police, and anyone else who considered it, were confused. The only predators in the area were dingoes which might attack a child, but not a full-grown man. Hairs left on the body were tested for DNA and came back as "wolf", an animal that should never have been in the Australian bush.

A thorough search showed found no wolf in the area. Wherever it had come from, wherever it went, it was not there any more. The mystery remained.

A month later, her uncle's solicitor contacted Karen to advise she had inherited the family property.

www.ingramcontent.com/pod-product-compliance
Lightning Source LLC
Chambersburg PA
CBHW070825250626
47170CB00006B/2209